THE **FORGIVE MY FINS** SERIES

Forgive My Fins
Fins Are Forever
Just for Fins
Pretty in Pearls

PRETTY IN PEARLS

PRETTY IN PEARLS

A FORGIVE MY FINS NOVELLA

TERA LYNN CHILDS

FEARLESS ALCHEMY

LAS VEGAS ▪ SERFOPOULA ▪ THALASSINIA ▪ ABYSSOS ▪ THE VEIL

Pretty in Pearls
a Forgive My Fins novella
Copyright © 2014 by Tera Lynn Childs

FEARLESS ALCHEMY
2232 South Nellis Boulevard, Suite 112
Las Vegas, NV 89104.
fearlessalchemy.com

This book is a work of fiction. Names, characters, places, and events are either products of the author's imagination or are used fictitiously, and any resemblance to actual persons, living or dead, businesses, events, or places is entirely coincidental.

ISBN 978-0-9861623-9-8 (paperback)
ISBN 978-0-9861623-6-7 (ebook)

Published in the United States of America.

The text type was set in Adobe Caslon Pro
Cover design by Tera Lynn Childs
Book design by Tera Lynn Childs

First Edition

PRETTY IN PEARLS

ONE

The Thalassinian Marketplace is, in my opinion, one of the wonders of the underwater world. Held on the open sands of the old town square, the market boasts vendors of every kind hawking their wares. Farmers come from the rural regions, beyond the edges of the city, with barrels of sweet smelling sand strawberries, fresh kelp, and pickled sea fans. Lobstermen put the fattest of their herd on display. Breathtaking bouquets, tasty delicacies, and even the odd salvage stall selling human treasures that have been found on the ocean floor—a mergirl could get lost in all the options.

But I know exactly where I'm going. I swim past the food and flower displays, over the organic sea-life stalls, and around the tables of trinkets. I make straight for my favorite vendor: Paru's Pearls.

Pearls are plentiful under the sea, and many girls consider them ordinary. Plain. Common. To me they will always be the most beautiful things in all the oceans. I love the way that some gleam and others sparkle. They come in all the colors of the rainbow, from bright white to soft pink to inky gray to the blackest black

I've ever seen.

I can't wait to browse the latest collection.

As I turn a corner, an older merwoman loses her grip on her shopping basket, sending a dozen live starfish tumbling across the aisle. I swerve out of the way as the woman dives after her lost bounty, then turn around to help. Most of the starfish remain within reach, and the woman quickly gathers them back. One is making a gallant bid for freedom.

I retrieve the wayward starfish and return it to the woman. "This one almost got away."

"Such a sweet dear." Her face crinkles into a bright smile. She reaches up and pinches my cheek. "Thank you."

I smile back before turning and continuing toward my destination. The pearls are calling.

I approach the stall, swimming with such momentum that I stop kicking and float the rest of the way. If I weren't so excited, I might have noticed the trio passing in front of the stall.

Of course I crash hardest into the meanest of the three.

"I'm so sorry," I blurt, kicking myself out of the way, out of reach. "I wasn't looking where I was—"

"Swim much?" Astria asks, sneering.

"Yeah," Piper chirps. "Swim much?"

Venus snorts.

I stare wide-eyed at the terrible trio. Astria, Piper, and Venus have been awful to me since guppihood. They take great delight in making me feel as small and worthless as possible. They try to belittle my best friend, too, but Lily is the princess. They can't be as cruel with her or there might be repercussions. With me, though, they act without restraint.

It doesn't help that they're gorgeous. Astria has beautiful red hair and perfect alabaster skin. Piper looks more like a California mermaid, with sunny, blond hair and a fake tan that almost matches her golden tail fin. Venus is the most exotic, with dark skin, waves of midnight curls, and rich mahogany scales.

I feel dim in their presence. With my boring brown hair and brown eyes, I practically fade into the shadows. Only my tail fin, a bright copper in a thousand shining shades, makes me feel special.

Looking down and away, I mutter another, "I'm sorry," and try to swim past.

Astria never lets me get away that easily.

"Shopping for pearls?" Her upper lip curls in a sneer. "Again?"

I just shake my head and dart into the stall. I hear them laughing and making fun as they swim off into the market. No matter how many times I tell myself not to let them win, their barbs and mockery always sting.

Closing my eyes, I take a deep, cleansing breath.

"You're better than those three put together," a male voice says.

Startled, I spin around. *Riatus.*

Usually Paru works the stall herself, with occasional help from her daughter Coral—who is a couple of years younger than me and just about the sweetest girl in all of Thalassinia. Pearl harvesting is a time-intensive business, and Paru can't spare any of her workers to hawk beads to tourists and shoppers when they could be gathering more.

On my last visit Paru told me she was leaving soon for a trading tour of the southern hemisphere. Off to seek out the rarest pearls ever found. She hadn't told me her son would be taking her place in the stall.

I haven't seen Riatus in over a year, not since he left on his grand adventure to explore the world's oceans and make contacts for the family business. His departure had been so sudden. One day he was in the stall, the next he was gone and Paru was telling me about his big trip.

My heart pounds and my breathing quickens. In a flash, my guppihood crush splashes back to life—years of pining and longing and excitement just to see a glimpse of him in the stall or when he delivered orders to the house.

He looks even more like a dashing pirate than he used to. His hair, black as squid ink, is longer and held back by a red-and-black scarf. Where it flows out the back, I can see tiny, silvery shells woven into his locks. His tail fin has darkened into a deep navy that fades to a green-blue at the bottom. I've been dreaming of those dark eyelashes and the pale silver eyes they frame since my first trip to the pearl stall with Mom all those years ago.

But today, it's his mouth, quirked up to one side, that I can't stop staring at.

"Wh-what?" I stammer.

He jerks his head after the terrible trio. "I've seen the likes of them plenty," he explains. "Your sort is worth ten of them." He winks. "At least."

"I—yeah—they—"

Come on, Peri, say something.

"Thanks," I finally manage with a lame smile.

He shakes his head and lowers his gaze as if it's no big deal.

When those pale eyes pause at the base of my throat, his grin widens. "That's beautiful," he says. "One of ours?"

With a gasp, my hand goes to my throat, to the spot where I know a big, fat pearl—the size of a ripe kelpberry and the exact coppery shade of my tail fin—hangs from a simple gold chain. He doesn't remember. Why would he?

One day, years and years ago, I'd been too sick to accompany Mom to the market. I was devastated, of course, because that meant missing a chance to see Riatus. Mom had the pearl order sent to our house and he had been the one to deliver it. I was asleep in bed when I heard a soft knock at my window.

Riatus was floating outside, a sheepish grin on his face.

"Here," he said as he handed me the pearl. "Feel better."

Then, without another word, he swam away.

We never spoke about that moment. I never even wore the pearl—I was too afraid he would know what it meant to me, and too afraid I would lose it—until he left on his adventure. I started wearing it as a reminder, a way to feel closer to him when he was who-knew-where in the world.

"Yes, one of *yours*," I answer cryptically. "It was a gift."

The bemused look on his face gives me more satisfaction than it probably should.

"Peri!" Coral whips across the stall and pulls me into a tight hug.

Riatus frowns. "Peri?"

"You remember Peri," Coral says, releasing me and spinning to her brother's side. "She's Mrs. Wentletrap's daughter."

His frown transforms into a wry smile. "Little Peri?"

My cheeks burn. This was always our problem—well, *my* problem. He's only two years older than me, but he makes it feel like a decade. A century. He sees me as the little guppy who comes to his stall with her mommy.

"She's emissary to the princess," Coral brags. "Not so little anymore."

I feel Riatus's pale gaze sweep over me from head to tail fin.

"Little Peri," he repeats, his expression turning curious, interested. "All grown-up."

His bemusement deepens as he realizes who I am. It's only been a year—I can't have changed *that* much—but I feel older, more mature. Maybe he sees that, too.

He studies me for what feels like ages even though I know it's only seconds. There is something different about how he is looking at me now, different from moments ago and different from before he left. Like I'm watching him mentally erase the "little" he used to place before my name.

"It's been a while," I say, trying to diffuse some of the tension. "How was your grand adventure?"

He smiles, but not before I notice a brief tension in his jaw. "Grand," he says vaguely. "How about you? Emissary to the princess—that's pretty impressive."

"She's my best friend." I shrug.

"She's not stupid," he argues. "You wouldn't have the position if you couldn't do the job."

Coral gasps. "Are you helping plan the Sea Harvest Dance?"

"No," I answer. "The dance committee is in charge of that."

"I hope I get to go this year." She twists into a dreamy swirl. "I hear it's magical."

"Is that coming up soon?" Riatus asks.

Coral stops and gapes at him. "In less than a *month*!"

"Hey, sea squirt," he says, playfully thumping her on the shoulder, "I've been gone for a year. I didn't know."

"But it's *always* the night of the August full moon," she replies. "Always."

She looks at me, as if seeking support.

"It is," I admit.

"Traitor," Riatus teases me, but there is no venom in his voice.

Coral starts dancing around us in a twirling spiral, lost in her dreams of the dance. It's true, the Sea Harvest Dance—the culminating event of the Sea Harvest Festival—is positively dreamy. Lily and I have gone together since we were old enough to attend. This year, though, she'll be going with Quince.

"Are you going?" Riatus asks. "To the dance."

My breath catches in my throat.

"Yes," I manage. "I mean, probably. I always do."

We float in silence—except for the sound of Coral humming as she dances. I'm trying not to stare at him—which is really, really hard when I haven't even *seen* him in a year. And he's . . . I don't know, trying to act like this isn't the most awkward moment ever.

"Are you?" I finally ask. "Going? To the dance?"

Lord love a lobster, when did I lose all ability to ask a complete question?

"I've never been," he says.

"Never?"

"But there's always a first time." He shrugs, a casual gesture, yet full of meaning. "I'm trying to make some changes in my life.

Maybe I'll start with the dance."

"Great," Coral exclaims, swimming up next to us and smacking us both on the shoulder. "You two go together. Now we just need to find *me* a date."

"What?" I stare at her like she's lost her mind. Turning to Riatus, I try to assure him that this was not my idea. I don't want him to think it's a setup or anything. "No, you don't have to. I mean, I didn't think you meant—"

"It's perfect, Peri," Coral says. "Do you have a date?"

"No," I admit. "But that doesn't mean—"

"And my brother has been gone for a year." She looks at him adoringly, batting her eyes. "He's practically a feral fish. How will he ever find a date in the next four weeks?"

My throat makes a noise that's some sort of cross between choking and crying. What has gotten into Coral? We're friends, sure, but I've never asked her to set me up with her brother. Maybe she knew about my crush. Maybe she's just trying to help me out.

Whatever the case, I just want to swim and hide. I've never been more mortified.

I force myself to look at Riatus.

If I expected outrage or amusement—maybe even disgust—I'm stunned when I see . . . blushing. He's not scoffing at Coral's suggestion. My jaw slacks as I realize he might have *actually* been getting ready to ask me to the dance.

I can't think, can't speak. Can barely breathe.

"I'm a genius." Coral applauds her efforts, her dark curls bouncing in the current. "You can thank me later."

Riatus shakes his head, but he's smiling. "I'll thank you to be—"

"Well, well," a male voice says, interrupting whatever Riatus was going to say, "if it isn't my old friend Riatus. It's been, what? A year?"

I see Riatus stiffen—his shoulders straighten and his jaw tightens. Slowly he turns to face the merman who is entering the stall from the other side.

He's a year or two older than Riatus, around twenty or twenty-one. And there is something . . . unsettling about him. What is it? His tail fin is nothing usual—a steely gray with no scars or markings. His hair is also gray. A soft gray he was born with, not that he earned with age. It's not quite short, but it's not long either. Like maybe he's only been growing it out for a little while.

He's wearing a dark jacket with lots of pockets and military details. A few ratty tears give him a tough look, but that isn't anything you couldn't get at any of five clothing shops in town.

"A year *exactly*," Riatus says, with little warmth in his voice. "What are you doing here, Prax?"

Maybe not such a good friend after all.

"I heard you were back in town," Prax says with a disarming smile. "I've missed you."

"I'm sure you have."

"And don't tell me," Prax says turning to face me, "this is Coral all grown-up."

There is something too familiar about his expression—way too familiar for anyone who confuses me for Coral. Behind him, I see Riatus's jaw clench even tighter. Whatever Prax is to him, he's not thrilled for him to be here.

Or for Prax to be paying attention to his sister.

Coral smacks him on the shoulder. "*I'm* Coral," she says. "That's Peri. She's my brother's friend. How come we've never met?"

"How come indeed?" Prax muses. "Let's remedy that right now. I'm Praxis Hake."

He extends his hand and, when she takes it, bows low before her. I try to meet Riatus's gaze and roll my eyes, but he is staring daggers into Prax's back.

"I'm Coral Ballenato." Her smile lights up the whole market.

Riatus's scowl could blow the whole place up.

"Excuse me, young man," a customer says, oblivious to the tense scene playing out here as she taps Riatus on the shoulder. "Could you help me choose a selection of pink pearls for my granddaughter's first necklace?"

"Of course, ma'am," he says, shedding his black mood in an instant. He turns to Coral. "Show her the Conch Shell Pink collection."

When she starts to argue, he adds, "Please."

"Fine," she says with a huff before swimming away.

The moment she is on the other side of the stall, he's in Prax's face.

"Leave. Her. Alone."

I shiver at the menace in his tone, and it's not even directed at me. For a girl without an older brother, it's exhilarating to see one so protective of his baby sister. I appreciate that, even if I don't understand what's going on here.

Maybe it's that Prax is several years older than Coral. Or maybe it's a guy thing, that they don't like friends hitting on their sisters. Who knows?

Prax lifts both hands in surrender. "I was just being nice. Don't go all great white on me."

"I don't care," Riatus snaps. "Coral is off-limits."

"Whatever, man." Prax smirks as he shrugs nonchalantly. His gaze drifts to me and his smile deepens. "Seems like you're surrounded by lovely, delicate merladies. I'm just trying to even the numbers."

Me? Delicate? Hardly.

With a single kick, Riatus shifts his position to place me kind of behind him—to place himself between me and Prax.

"Leave Peri out of this, too."

"Look, I can take a hint," Prax says, floating back. He looks at me over Riatus's shoulder. "Nice to meet you, Peri. I hope we run into each other again *soon*."

I smile because I'm not sure what the right response is. Clearly Riatus has a problem with him, but I don't know what. Prax nods and then, before I can figure out if I should say something, anything, he swims away.

Riatus turns to face me with an apologetic smile. "I'm sorry about that."

"It's no big deal," I say. "Obviously you have a history and—"

"Ri, which ones are South Pacific," Coral calls out, "and which ones are Indian Ocean?"

"Just a sec," he answers over his shoulder. Then, to me, "I'd better help her."

"Yeah, I need to get going anyway," I say quickly. "With all of Mom's preparations for the Sea Harvest Dance, I'm sure I'll be around again soon."

Even if she doesn't need me to visit.

"I'm counting on it," he says.

I can't quite bring myself to swim away just yet, letting my eyes follow him across the stall. Which means I'm caught staring when he turns back around. "Hey," he says with a half smile, "I'll bubble message you."

"Great!"

As Riatus swims away to help Coral with the customer, I'm overflowing with excitement. When I left home this morning, I had no idea what the market would have in store for me. I'm not usually a big fan of surprises. This kind, though, I could get used to.

TWO

Two weeks later

Normally I can't think of anything better than spending a day shopping in the market with my best friend. Especially with the Sea Harvest Dance only two weeks away. Stall owners are quick to pull out their very best offerings to tempt the princess, hoping to present something she might want to eat, wear, or show off on a shelf.

To them she is the future queen.

To me she will always be Lily.

But today, the market is the last place I want to be. I only agreed to come so I wouldn't have to explain why.

"Oh my gosh, Peri, look at this," Lily says, swimming into a stall of silks imported from the Indian Ocean. I give it a less than a minute before the owner realizes the princess is in his stall.

She pulls a silk off the rack. A ribbon of soft orange ripples in the current, the gold trim and beaded embroidery glittering as it catches the sunlight filtering down from the surface.

"It's beautiful." I catch the cloth between my fingers. "High-quality, too."

"You should buy it," she says, holding it up next to my face.

I make a face and shake my head.

"It's perfect for your coloring." She gives me that sunny grin that no one can deny. "You have to."

Maybe she's right, but it's not my favorite color. I'm shaking my head when the owner appears from behind another rack.

"Welcome, welcome," he says. "What brings you to—oh!"

Thirty whole seconds. I bite back a smile. Here we go.

He bows deeply, displaying his balding head. "Princess," he says, his voice full of reverence, "it is an honor."

"Thank you," Lily replies. "Your silks are beautiful."

He whips upright. "These are nothing. Let me show you my special collection."

In a flash, he's gone, diving behind the counter to find the best silks to show the princess. Lily gives me an apologetic look. She gets embarrassed by the attention, but after a lifetime of being her friend, I'm used to it. Mom and I have been buying silks for her dressmaking business from Mr. Egregia forever. He hasn't even noticed I'm in the stall.

Such is the life of a princess's best friend.

"Ah, yes," he exclaims, popping up from behind the counter with an armful of fabric. "Here we go."

Lily and I swim over to the counter as he lays them out. They are truly breathtaking. There is a shiny one—cross woven with lime green and gold—that would match Lily's tail fin perfectly. Mom would love the lavender one embroidered with white and purple flowers. But me? I reach for the ivory silk. It looks ordinary at first glance, just a stretch of off-white cloth. But as the current catches it, the fabric ripples and the glittery finish catches the light. A sparkling dream.

"Wow, that's amazing," Lily says, swimming over to take a closer look.

"The lady has excellent taste," Mr. Egregia says, finally looking at me. "Ah, Miss Wentletrap. I should have known."

His smile is broad and genuine.

"Hello, Mr. Egregia." I lift the glittery silk. "Is this what I think it is?"

"Silica-infused dupioni," he says, confirming my hunch.

"The process to make this is so involved," I explain to Lily, "they only make twenty yards a year."

"And I have secured ten of them," he boasts.

"You're holding out on my mom," I tease. "You know she loves this fabric."

"It arrived but yesterday." He looks flustered, like he thinks I'm actually mad. "I would sell to none other."

Sometimes it backfires when I try for sarcasm. I should probably stop trying. I give him a reassuring smile. "She will be so happy."

He looks relieved.

"I think I have to buy this one," Lily says, pointing at the green-and-gold I knew she would love. "Can you have it sent to the palace?"

Mr. Egregia bows again. "It would be an honor."

Moments later the arrangements are made and Lily and I are swimming off in search of another treasure.

"Where do you want to go next?" she asks.

"This is your shopping expedition," I reply, linking my arm through hers. "Where do *you* want to go?"

"Hmmmm, let me see . . ."

Her voice has that high, singsongy quality that indicates trouble brewing. I brace myself.

"How about Paru's Pearls?" she suggests. "I'm sure we could find *something* to look at there."

I knew this was coming. When Lily asked me to go shopping—not normally on her top thousand things to do—I had a feeling she was up to something. Now I know.

"That's all the way on the other side of the market," I argue. "We should just work our way over there."

Lily huffs. "But what if they sell out?"

"They won't," I insist.

She gives me a pleading look. "They might."

"They literally have *barrels* of pearls." I stare straight ahead, determined not to let her puppy-dog face sway me. "They won't sell out."

She unlinks our arms and turns to face me, arms crossed over her chest. The determined look in her eyes worries me. A determined Lily is not easily discouraged. Just ask Brody—the boy she crushed on for three long years before realizing that Quince was her true love.

"What's going on?" she demands.

I feign ignorance. "What do you mean?'

"I mean," she says, lowering her voice as she swims closer, "that two weeks ago you were all swoony over . . . Paru's Pearls, and now you're acting like you don't even want to . . . check out their stock."

"Their stock?" I echo with a half laugh.

She scowls. "You know what I mean."

I do—and we both know we're not talking about pearls—but that doesn't mean I want to talk about it. She's my best friend and I talk to her about everything. Almost everything. Not this.

A lot can happen in two weeks. A lot can change.

"Really, Lily," I say, swimming back a few inches, acting like I simply want to keep shopping, "I have no idea what you're talking about. You've been spending too much time on land. It's like you're speaking a foreign language."

I swim off before she can respond, heading for the nearest stall as cover. Because the truth is, I know exactly what—exactly *who*— she's talking about. And the last thing I want to talk about is him.

Three hours, eighteen stalls, matching beaded braids, and a very full lunch later, my time runs out. I knew I could only delay for so long, that eventually we would make our way to this back corner of the market.

If nothing else, I knew Lily would make sure we did.

As we kick into Paru's Pearls, a stall overflowing with iridescent orbs, my stomach does a triple flip. One flip of excitement to see what new pearls will be on display. One flip of excitement to see him. A final flip of dread that he will act just as casually uninterested as he has the last five times I visited the stall.

You'd think I would stop coming.

But no, I'm a glutton for punishment, it seems. Especially if that punishment involves getting to look at him for even a few seconds.

"You want to tell me what happened?" Lily asks as we float over to the nearest display.

I trace my fingers over the field of pale blue pearls. "Not really."

"Come on," Lily urges, swimming close enough to whisper. "I can't help if I don't know what happened. And because right now, to be honest, you're acting a little crazy."

I *am* acting crazy. What is wrong with me? I'm usually a very together sort of mergirl. That's why I'm Lily's emissary—basically her personal assistant—because I can keep my head on straight and make sure she knows everything she needs to know before state events.

This? Freaking out over a boy and feeling completely adrift? This is not normal Peri behavior.

Neither is thinking about myself in the third person. I need serious intervention. No, I need to tell my best friend what's happened.

I draw in a deep breath and let it out in a long sigh. She's going to find out eventually. I might as well get it over with.

In a tight whisper, I begin, "Well, you know I've had a crush on Riatus for, like, ever."

Lily nods enthusiastically.

"Two weeks ago," I continue, "when he was first back from his swim around the world, it seemed like he was finally going to see me as something other than the little mergirl who shopped in his stall. It seemed like he might actually be interested in me, like he might actually ask me to the Sea Harvest Dance. My dreams were finally coming true."

"I know," Lily says too loudly. I glare at her and she continues at a lower volume, "You seemed so happy. So excited. I knew it was something good."

"Right," I say, my shoulders slumping. "Then the next time I went back, it was like an iceberg crashed into his heart. He wasn't rude or anything; he was just . . . polite. Distant. Like we'd never met."

"Like how?"

"Like . . . he smiled politely, chatted politely, helped me—"

"Politely?" she suggests.

"Yes," I say. "He's been exactly the same ever since."

"That's so weird," she says.

Don't I know it?

No bubble message. No date to the dance. No acknowledgment that maybe, for a moment, he kind of thought he might be interested in me as more than a mergirl who shops in his stall. Nothing.

"Well, forget him. He doesn't deserve you," Lily says, cheering me like only a best friend can. "You're so much better than him."

"I know," I say in a small voice.

But that doesn't mean I don't still want to know why, doesn't mean I don't still want *him*. I sigh again.

"Don't let him ruin our expedition," she says, swimming into the stall. "You love pearl shopping."

She's right. But for today, I can abstain. I keep to the edge, hoping that maybe I'll be able to see him without him noticing me.

"Peri?" a male voice says from right behind me.

Great. Clearly that hope was futile.

I wish my skin didn't tingle at the sound of him saying my name. I wish I could remember how he's all but ignored me since that first meeting that had seemed so . . . promising. I wish I could think about anything other than the fact that I can feel his warmth, even through the chilly water.

Time to be a big girl. I paste a friendly smile on my face and turn to face him. "Hi, Riatus."

Those pale silver eyes seem to glow as they watch me. But his mouth is pursed slightly, like he's irritated that I'm here.

Well, I'm irritated that he's irritated.

I don't know what I did or what made him change his mind about me, but it's pretty hard to ditch feelings for someone just because they lose interest.

Which is why my heart is beating faster than normal.

For an instant, I see something in his pale eyes that is far from disinterest. Then it's gone and he's back to the vaguely charming boy who treats me like nothing more than just another customer.

"What can I help you with today?" he asks.

I force my fake smile to get even bigger. "Just browsing. Thanks."

"Come look at these, Peri," Lily calls out from across the stall.

I brush past him. "Excuse me."

Joining Lily at a tray full of the whitest pearls I have ever seen, I feign interest in the display, doing my best to ignore Riatus.

"Aren't they gorgeous?" Lily asks, waving her fingers over the pearls.

"They're called Arctic Ice." I pick one up for a closer look. "They're harvested in Glacialis."

Lily and I visited the northernmost kingdom in the Western Atlantic once on an official mission, and I did all of the background research. I'd been fascinated to learn about the pearls, known to be the purest white in all the seven seas.

They are so bright they are rumored to glow like a beacon in the dark.

"They are harvested once a year," Riatus explains, either *not* interested in letting me pretend to be indifferent to him or *more* interested in showing off his stock. "In the heart of winter, when the Arctic seas are at their coldest."

"Fascinating," Lily says.

I glare at Riatus across the display, but he isn't looking at Lily or the pearls or even my face. His gaze—fierce and intense, icy gray—is focused on the base of my throat.

"What?" I whisper as my hand goes to my neck, certain to find the remains of lunch—sea-cucumber jelly or lobsterman's pie—stuck to my skin.

Instead, I feel the necklace dangling there. Wearing it became such a habit in the past year, I totally forgot it was even there.

"I just . . ." I want to give him some explanation, some reason other than the truth—that the pearl means more to me than I want him to know. But nothing comes out. It's hard to come up with a convincing lie when the truth is so blatantly on display.

Then, before the moment can get anymore awkward than it already is, he turns to Lily.

"Here, Princess," he says, "let me show you the golden collection. I'm sure we have a selection to complement your scales."

I let out a rough breath. What was I thinking? That he recognized the pearl? That he remembered giving it to me? No way. He made that clear when we first saw each other again two weeks ago. Why did I think he would have suddenly remembered?

Still, the water between him and me? More than a little tense.

When Lily and I swim out of the stall twenty minutes later, she has a shopping bag full of pearls—beautiful gold ones I know Mom will want to use on the princess's dress for the Sea Harvest Dance—and I have progressed from utterly confused to downright flicked off.

"I'm not crazy," I say.

Lily looks up from her bag of pearls. "Did I say you were?"

"I mean, if a boy flirts with you, if he tells you he's going to bubble message you"—I absently rub the pearl at my throat—"that should mean he's interested. Right?"

Lily nod. "Totally!"

"That was weird. Wasn't that weird?" I spin around to face her. "You felt it, too. Right?"

Lily studies me, an angelfish on her face. She's probably amused to see me so worked up over a boy, but right now I can't even manage to be indignant about that. I just want advice.

"What do I do?" I demand.

"What do you do?" She smiles. "I think . . ." she says, drawing it out until I'm practically leaning forward in anticipation.

Lily may not have the most exhaustive experience with boys. There's the boy she crushed on for three years—who barely knew she existed and is now bonded with her cousin Dosinia—and then there's Quince. Who is, to be fair, pretty much every mergirl's dream wrapped up in one tidy, biker-boy package.

But still, her advice is better than no advice, and she knows me better than anyone.

" . . . you need . . ."

I hold my breath.

" . . . to talk to him."

I'm not sure what I imagined her advice was going to be, but that was not it.

"Talk to him?" I echo.

She nods. "Ask him what's going on."

"Ask him?" I shake my head. "I can't just ask him."

"Of course you can." She smiles. "You have a right to know. I mean, he all but asked you to the dance, right?"

"Right, but—"

"Then ask him why he didn't." She places her hands on my shoulders. "You still like him, obviously. What do you have to lose? Ask him."

She makes it sound so simple. Just swim up to him and say, Hey, you said you were going to bubble message me and I thought you might ask me to the dance and then you started treating me like a total stranger. What's up with that? Have a personality change or something?

Oh yeah, sure, I'll just ask him.

"Even better," Lily says excitedly, "why don't *you* ask *him* to the dance?"

"What?" I cough.

She swings her arms wide, a huge smile on her face. "Absolutely. Ask Riatus to the dance. I bet you'll be surprised by the answer."

I frown at her.

Bet I won't.

THREE

After much thought and consideration—and prodding from Lily—I relent and decide to try talking to Riatus. But not until after the market closes for the day. I can't imagine anything more awkward than asking a guy whether he likes you or not in front of a crowd of shoppers.

After the sun sets, replaced by the bioluminescent glow that keeps Thalassinia from ever being completely dark, I sneak back through the aisles of the market.

Most of the stall keepers are packing up their goods for the night—covering the food and flower displays, packing the organic sea life into storage bins, placing valuable trinkets into locked chests.

I've never seen this side of the market. It's like staying in the ballroom after the royal party, when the palace staff starts taking down the displays to return everything to normal. An insider's peek into a secret world.

As I approach the back corner of the market, my heart starts racing, fast. Like, I have to stop and catch my breath and make sure I'm not having a panic attack.

But no, after a minute of slow breathing, my heart gets back under control. I give myself a couple extra minutes, just to make sure, before pushing out from behind a rack of seaflower fascinators and continuing on my way.

I round the last corner and freeze.

Coral is still in the stall too. I hadn't counted on that. All my imaginings had me swimming up on Riatus alone. I need a minute to regroup.

As I watch, Riatus is moving the barrels of pearls to the back of the stall, probably so he can lock down all the lids and secure the whole collection to the seahorse hitching post in the back corner.

I notice Coral reach for something behind the counter and pull out a folded sheet of kelpaper. She opens it, scans the contents, and laughs out loud.

Riatus turns, probably to ask her what's so funny, and she quickly hides the note behind her back. She says something that leaves him shaking his head. A moment later, she darts forward, places a kiss on his cheek, and then swims away, out of the stall—out of the market. The kelpaper drifts away behind her and lands on one of the barrels.

This is my chance. Riatus is alone. I should swim over there and ask my questions. He goes back to work, dancing around the stall as he moves the barrels into position. There is something so boyish, so joyful about his movements. I have to watch for a minute longer.

I can't breathe, and this time it has nothing to do with freaking out. It has everything to do with him.

Holy hammerhead.

When he's nudged the last barrel into place next to the others, he starts locking them down. I watch, hypnotized by his quick, precise movements. It only takes him a few seconds to finish them all. Then he's dragging a thick chain through the rings and locking them to the post.

As he drifts back a little, swiping a hand across the back of his neck, I know it's time to act. He's done for the night. I have to go now, or he'll head home and I'll have to languish another day.

I would never hear the end of it from Lily.

I flex my tail fin, ready to kick myself over to the stall, when I see him find the piece of kelpaper Coral let float to the ground. He reads whatever's written on the paper, his scowl deepening as he goes. Crumpling up the paper, he looks like he wants to throw it into the open sea. Instead, he grabs his jacket from the corner and stuffs the paper into a pocket.

Then he pulls the jacket on. He's leaving.

The time for hiding and excuses is over. Time to use up all my courage and ask that boy if he wants to go to the Sea Harvest Dance with me.

I kick out from behind the counter just in time to see Riatus swimming away in the opposite direction.

Oh no. He can't get away that easily. I'm going to talk to him tonight if I have to follow him all the way to the mainland.

With determination stiffening my spine, I swim off after him.

Riatus is fast. When I took off after him, I figured I would be able to keep up pretty easily. He wasn't swimming a merathon, after all.

But as soon as he clears Old Town he kicks it into high gear, and I'm swimming for my life to keep up. It's fast becoming a matter of pride to not let him get away.

We're swimming over the oldest structures in town, through the eastern suburbs, and out into the open ocean before I realize we're leaving the city.

I dive lower, toward the ocean floor. I know my goal is to talk to him—which generally requires him knowing that I'm in the vicinity—but right now the last thing I want is for him to see me chasing after him like a crazy merperson.

We pass an ancient signpost and I finally figure out where he's heading. Once we clear the rocky outcropping ahead, we'll be at the edge of the Black Kelpforest.

I was fifteen before I even had courage to look at the Black Kelpforest, let alone approach the edge. Parents like to frighten little merchildren by telling them stories about the sharks and sea monsters that live in there.

The reality is almost worse. Only black-market traders, poachers, and criminals visit the forest. Thalassinia is one of the safest kingdoms in all the oceans, but the Black Kelpforest is the one place where nasty things happen regularly. It's a rare week that goes by without news of something illegal and usually violent happening here.

This idea just went from bad to catastrophic.

I need to turn back. I know this. I tell myself this. Repeatedly.

A voice in the back of my mind—a voice that sounds remarkably like Lily's—urges me to keep going just a little farther.

Riatus disappears over the outcropping, dropping down out of sight. I slow as I approach the edge. Stopping at the top, I peer over and watch him swim for the edge of the forest.

He's really going in. What possible reason could he have for racing out of town and venturing into the darkest, scariest forest in Thalassinia at this time of night?

This is nuts.

I've taken this too far. It's definitely time to turn around and head back for the safety of town.

I watch for a few seconds longer—to make sure he's really, *really* going into the forest—before turning away to start the swim back.

Only as I turn, my tail fin knocks into a loose rock and sends it soaring out over the edge. Sinking swiftly and spiraling toward Riatus far below. I dash out, desperate to grab it before it falls to the ocean floor.

I'm too slow.

The rock swooshes out of my reach and I watch in horror as the current sends it swirling and twisting. What if it hits him? I should bolt, should get myself out of here before the rock hits the floor. But I can't.

Instead, I'm floating like an idiot, staring at Riatus as the rock lands with a spray of sand.

He doesn't turn at first, and I think maybe he won't notice. Maybe he didn't feel the disturbance in the water. Maybe—maybe—luck is actually on my side.

Then he turns around.

Looks up.

I know the exact moment he sees and recognizes me. His eyes widen for a moment and then narrow into an angry scowl. Even across the distance between us I can feel his fury.

Jeez, I know it's a little weird—in a crazy, psycho, stalker-chick way—that I've followed him out here to the edge of the forest. But does he really have to—

"Oh boy."

Riatus pushes off from the floor and swims for me. I'm not sure what makes me turn and flee. It could be the look on his face. It could be natural preservation instinct. It could be I'm totally humiliated and horrified to be caught following a merboy I barely know into the most dangerous part of our kingdom.

Whatever the reason, I turn around and swim for home as fast as I can.

Riatus is faster.

If I thought he was hightailing it on the way here, he is a freaking speed demon now. Before I am five fin flicks away, he zooms past me, whips around, and swirls himself to a stop in my path. I react instantly, altering my course to swim off to my right. I don't know where I'm going, but I'm going there fast.

"Peri!" He's not far behind me.

I spot a little grove of lacelike sea fans ahead of me, and I streamline. Kicking as hard as I can, I make it to the grove ahead of him. Maybe the sea fans will give me some cover. Their thick trunks and intricately branching limbs make it almost impossible to see inside. Maybe he'll be so focused on chasing after me he won't realize I've diverted.

With my back up against the tallest, thickest sea fan in the bunch, I try to slow my panting so he can't hear me. I'm not scared—it wasn't that kind of chase. It's not like I think Riatus is going to hurt me. I'm embarrassed. I'm horrifically, hysterically embarrassed.

Why did I think I should—

"What in the seven seas are you doing?"

Riatus appears in front of me. It's only a small concession that he is panting as hard as I am.

"What are you doing here?" he demands. "Were you following me?"

"No!" Stupid answer. "Yes. I mean, I didn't mean to."

"Didn't mean to?"

I shake my head. "I just wanted to talk to you."

He throws his head back and stares up toward the surface, like he'll find some kind of answer there.

"I was waiting for you to finish closing down for the night. I didn't want to interrupt," I say, trying to fill the silence and explain my actions. "Then you read some note and took off, and I—"

He gaze swings back to me. Those pale gray eyes spear me with intensity.

"You have no idea what you're getting into," he says.

His brows are furrowed so deeply there are twin lines in the center of his forehead. He looks . . . scared.

For the first time I realize I might have gotten myself into a really bad situation. Okay, not for the first time, because I knew this was a stupid thing to do from the beginning, but now the danger seems real.

"I—I'm sorry," I stammer, trying to back away—only to realize I'm pressed up against a huge sea-fan trunk. Brilliant plan. "I shouldn't have come, shouldn't have followed you."

"No," he says, floating closer into my personal space. "You shouldn't have."

"I should go."

He kicks closer still, and braces his hands on the sea fan at either side of my shoulders. He's so close I can make out the specks of sky blue at the centers of his eyes. I can see the faint freckles that dust his cheeks and forehead. I can feel his heat and I can't suppress a shiver.

"Forget you ever followed me," he says. He hesitates, scowls like he's thinking about saying something more, but doesn't.

Instead, he floats back, giving me enough space to get away. That more than anything gives me the courage to ask, "Is it something illegal?"

I could forgive a lot of things. If it's something stupid or risky or totally-innocuous-and-I'm-overreacting, then that's fine. But as emissary to the princess, I can't condone illegal activities. How hypocritical would that be?

The muscles in his jaw tighten and his nostrils flare. "Of course not."

"Of course not?" I spit back before I can think. "There's no 'of course not' about it. You just raced out of town to the edge of the Black Kelpforest—aka the epicenter of all criminal activity in Thalassinia—under cover of darkness. I think illegal activity is a totally legitimate guess on my part."

He watches me finish my rant. I can't tell if he thinks I'm gutsy or stupid—or both. Then, after an increasingly uncomfortable silence, he barks out a deep laugh.

"Poseidon help me, Peri, but you are a fearless one."

I cross my arms over my chest, not sure if that's supposed to be a compliment or just an observation. It doesn't seem like a condemnation, so I choose to take it as a compliment. "Thank you."

He shakes his head, his smile fading. "There is nothing illegal about my activities tonight," he says. "I promise you."

His promise shouldn't mean anything to me. I barely know him. He's just a cute boy who works in his mother's market stall. But for some reason, the words reassure me. There's a heaviness to them. A gravity.

I believe him, and I believe he takes his promises seriously.

That faith gives me the courage to ask the question that started this whole adventure. "Did I do something wrong after that first day in the market?"

He scowls, probably confused by my apparent change of subject. "I'm sorry?"

"I thought . . . I mean you seemed . . ." I sound like an idiot. "You said you would message me."

His pale eyes study me. "I did."

"But you haven't," I say. "So I must have done something to make you *not* want to."

"Peri—"

"It's okay," I interrupt. "I don't blame you. I mean, it's your prerogative, right? But I'd just like to know. For next time."

His eyes darken and his whole demeanor changes. His muscles tighten; his mouth lifts up just a tiny bit at the corners. He swims back closer to me and when he speaks his voice is both gentle and rough.

"You did nothing wrong."

He reaches up and brushes a lock of hair off my forehead. Sparks tingle across my whole body.

"It's the oldest excuse in the ocean," he continues. "But this time it's true. It's not you, it's me."

I want to roll my eyes—it *is* the oldest excuse in the whole world—but he didn't say it casually. He said it like it hurt.

"No matter how much I might want to go out with you," he says, "right now I just can't."

That should make me feel better. At least it's not something I did or didn't do. If anything was going to send him swimming for the hills, it would probably be my lovely display of stalkerish behavior tonight, and that's only a recent development in our non-relationship.

But it wasn't me, and somehow that makes me feel worse. Because no matter how much I wanted it, no matter how much I worried about whether he liked me or even how much he actually did, it made no difference. He just . . . *can't*.

I feel the first tickle of tears and I know I need to get out of there before my brown eyes start sparkling like shiny copper and he sees exactly how much that confession hurt. So I lower my gaze, nod a couple times—either in understanding or saying good-bye—and I swim away.

The tears start for real when I realize he's going to let me go.

I dash out of there—eager to start the long swim home before Riatus follows me out—and am just clearing the edge of the grove when something iridescent drifts into my peripheral vision. No, no, no. My heart starts racing again—this time I'm sure it is a panic attack—as I slowly turn to confirm my fears.

Floating a few feet away to my right is a jellyfish the size of great white shark.

Stay calm.

I turn back the other way, only to find another jellyfish floating even closer. I spin around in a full circle, desperate for a way out. But I'm surrounded. On all sides, including above. I'm caught in a jellyfish bloom.

And I know I'm going to die.

FOUR

"I *thought you* were leaving?" Riatus asks.

Jellyfish, jellyfish, jellyfish.

My mind can't think of anything but the swarm of massive, deadly beasts that have me trapped. In some deep corner of my mind, I know that they are not close enough, dense enough to have me literally trapped. But I can't move. I retreat, like always, into my panic.

"Peri," he says, his voice growing fainter even though he must be swimming closer, "you need to go home."

It happened when I was just a guppy, barely six years old. My family had gone to the Sea Star Amusement Park for the day. On the way home, my baby brother started chasing after me with a dead squid. We swam too far, not paying attention to where we were going, and before we knew it we were at the center of a smack even bigger than this one.

He died almost instantly.

I clung to life long enough for my parents to get me to the hospital. Physical recovery took a long time. Emotional recovery is still kind of a work in progress.

"Peri, what's wrong?"

Riatus's face drifts into my hazy vision. I try to focus on him, on his pretty, pale eyes and his dark, slashing brows. He looks worried. I don't want him to worry. Not about me.

I go through this every time. I know I do, I know I shouldn't, and I'm still helpless to stop.

He looks up and to the left, behind me. "Oh carp."

He's seen them.

His hands wrap around my upper arms. "I'm going to get you out of here," he says. "Slow and steady. Okay?"

I nod, because that's the only response I can manage.

He pulls me close, up against his body. One arm moves to wrap around my waist. It's so strong and secure that I actually feel a little better. Like I can breathe a little more.

Only when I drag in a deep breath, it pushes my chest into his.

That causes a whole different kind of reaction.

In a gentle, fluid movement, Riatus waves his tail fin. The movement sends us floating. Panic rises. What if he calculates wrong? What if he's sending us right into the deadly tentacles? What if we get caught in them and their stingers spear into our flesh, overloading our nervous systems with their paralyzing toxins?

My breathing speeds up and my vision starts to close in around me.

"I've got you," Riatus says, his voice gentle and soothing. "We're going to be fine."

His fingertips brush my cheek. I close my eyes, narrowing my focus to his touch. Putting all of my faith into him, putting his life in my hands. And I trust him.

I put my cheek against his chest. Every movement ripples through his body, against me, rocking me gently. It's soothing. Calming.

"Almost there," he whispers next to my ear.

I lose myself in the rhythmic movement. I push everything else out of my mind and focus on him, on the feeling of his body next to mine and the certainty that he will get me out of this alive. He will get *us* out of this alive.

I'm not sure how much time passes before he stops.

"You're okay." He releases my waist and I shiver against the chill.

I feel his palms on my cheeks, cupping my face in such a tender gesture that it breaks down my resolve to not cry. The tears build up behind my eyelids faster than I can stop them.

"Come back to me, angelfish," he whispers. "It's over now."

I shake my head against the emotion coursing through me. If I open my eyes now, if I let him see what I'm feeling, there will be no going back.

Then I feel his lips on my forehead. Firm and warm.

I melt.

When I open my eyes, I know they must look like glittering pennies. I don't care.

"Hey there." His smile lights up the whole ocean. "Welcome back."

The most amazing thing is that I don't feel embarrassed. I usually feel horrified after my panic attacks—what kind of freak just totally freezes up like that? As if turning into a statue does anything to help me survive a jellyfish bloom.

But with Riatus I feel only relief.

"Thank you," I say.

He drops his hands back to his side. "I remember hearing about the attack."

Everyone heard about it. My dad was a member of the king's cabinet. When bad things happen to kingdom officials, word gets around.

"You must have been, what?" he asks. "Seven?"

"Six," I reply. "I was six." I roll my shoulders, self-conscious of the scars that crisscross my back beneath the veil of my hair. Sometimes I still feel the sting. "My brother—he . . ."

My throat tightens and I can't say the words.

Riatus nods. "I'm sorry."

I bite my lip, keep back the emotion. "Thanks."

We fall silent for several long moments. I'm trying to process all the emotion about the past and about what just happened. I have no clue what Riatus is thinking. Hopefully not that I'm the craziest mergirl he's ever run into.

"I shouldn't have followed you," I say.

He looks back over his shoulder, back the way we came from. Right. Because not only am I the crazy mergirl who followed him halfway across town and turned into a basket case at the first sign of jellyfish, I'm also the crazy mergirl who ruined whatever plans took him to the Black Kelpforest in the first place.

Besides, he made it abundantly clear in the prejellyfish conversation that he's not interested in a relationship—not able, whatever.

"I should go." I scan the area, looking for a familiar landmark and finding none. "Where are we?"

"Halfmoon Harbor is right over that ridge," he says, pointing to a rocky hill a short ways behind me.

The suburban neighborhood is on the southeast corner of town. From there it's a short swim back to my home just outside the palace walls. I can be in my bed, this whole crazy disaster of a night a distant memory, in half an hour.

"See you around," I say, even though I really hope I don't. I'm barely keeping control of my humiliation at this point. I'm not looking forward to testing my resolve.

He doesn't say anything, and doesn't look like he's going to say anything, so I turn and start for the ridge.

"Hey, Peri," he says.

I whip back around way faster than any mergirl should, especially one who's trying to act like she doesn't care that the merboy she's crushing on is completely uninterested should. Way to play it uncool.

"Yeah?" My heart is pounding.

He gives me a tortured half smile. "Swim safe."

Seriously? My shoulders slump. *Swim safe?* That's the best he can do?

"Sure," I reply. "You too."

Then, before he can say something else to embarrass or infuriate me, I turn and swim for home. "Swim safe?" I mutter to myself. "Kiss my tail fin."

Now, if only I really meant it.

Being an emissary to a princess isn't the toughest job in the world. When that princess is your best friend, it's pretty much the greatest.

Basically it's up to me accompany Lily on royal visits to other kingdoms, prepare her with all the background information for the meetings, and step in as a go-between if necessary. She's going on a goodwill visit to Acropora next month and we're getting an early start on the prep work.

Acropora borders Thalassinia to the south, and they have suffered from the effects of ocean warming more than any kingdom. Lily and Quince have masterminded a huge aid network to help all the kingdoms of the western Atlantic cope with the reality of climate change. Since she is bonded—in name only—to Acropora's prince, Lily takes their welfare extra seriously.

"I want to be sure to check in on the new aid warehouse," she says. "It should be up and running at full capacity."

"Okay, I'll add it to your agenda." I write it down, after the meetings with Prince Tellin and King Gadus, but before the Marine Flora Expo. "Do you want to take any gifts for the royal family?"

"Oh, I should, shouldn't I?"

I nod. "It's customary."

Lily hangs her head back over her chair. "You're so much better at this kind of delicate politics."

"I'm not," I insist.

But we both know I am. It's one of the reasons the king assigned me as Lily's emissary. That, and the fact that I've always been interested in politics and royal law. Something I think I inherited from my dad.

"What about a harvest wreath?" I suggest. "I could be a nice symbol of sharing the wealth of our harvest with them."

"Perfect," Lily says.

I scribble down a note to order a wreath from Florella's Flowers. She has the best selection in all of Thalassinia and she's a small business. She can always use the extra orders.

"So, anything else?" I ask as I finish the note.

"I think that's everything." Lily floats back into her chair. "Can you think of anything we've missed?"

I set my notebook down on the desk. "No, but I'm sure I'll think of twenty things as soon as I get home."

"Good, now that business is over," Lily says, steepling her hands in front of her like some kind of supervillain, "you can tell me what happened with Riatus yesterday."

I slump back in my chair and huff out a frustrated breath that sends my bangs swirling. It was only a matter of time. Lily is not one to just let things go, especially when my love life—or lack thereof—is involved.

Since finding Quince it's like she's been on a mission to get me someone equally awesome.

But what can I tell her? That I stalked him across town and to the outer edges of civilization? That he went into the sketchiest part of Thalassinia, but promised me that he's not involved in anything illegal?

Because of her position, she might feel obligated to investigate even the hint of illegal behavior. I believed Riatus when he told me he wasn't a criminal, but Lily wouldn't have to. It would only take a few innocent questions to completely disrupt his life. And for him to realize that I totally ran and tattled to the princess.

No, I won't treat him as poorly as he's treated me, so I stick to the critical parts of the story.

"He said he couldn't go out with me," I admit. "That even if he wanted to, he just couldn't."

"Couldn't?" Lily leans forward, letting her elbows rest on her desk. "What does that even mean?"

"Honestly, I have no idea."

She gives me an impatient look. "Did you ask him?"

"No, I—" I tilt back to study her ceiling. "There were jellyfish."

"What?" Her green eyes soften with sympathy. "Are you okay?"

Lily knows my history, so she knows all about my panic fog. She's saved me from my frozen reaction more than once.

"I'm fine," I insist. "Riatus saved me."

She smiles, and I know he just earned a bunch of points with her. "I didn't see any reports of jellyfish in the marketplace."

"They weren't in the marketplace." Great, this is the part of the story where I have to tread carefully. "He was, um, leaving the market when I got there and I had to follow him."

"How far?" she asks.

My gaze remains fixed on her ceiling, counting the seashells in the intricately carved pattern. I feel the current move and I know she's not behind her desk anymore.

She appears above me, blocking the view to my distraction.

"How far, Peri?" she repeats. "To their warehouse?"

I shake my head, trying to avoid eye contact.

"To his home?"

If only. "No," I say with another shake. "Past the edge of town."

"Periwinkle Wentletrap!"

"What?" I finally look her in the eye. "He's a fast swimmer. And

I was determined to talk to him last night so I could ask him about the dance. And so that a certain princess wouldn't bug me about it forever."

I don't expect her to smile, and when she laughs I'm worried that she's gone over the edge. Yes, I'm pathetic and ridiculous. I don't expect my best friend to be so amused.

"It's all your fault," I say. "If I'm a crazy stalker, I'm using you as my defense in court."

She laughs even harder. "I am the court!"

"I'll ask for the king to preside," I retort. "He's always liked me."

After a few more laughs, Lily finally calms back to normal. She studies me, her green eyes serious and intent. It's like she's trying to read my brain.

If I weren't trapped in a chair I'd back away a few inches.

"What?"

"You like him." She takes my hands in hers and twirls me out of the chair. "You *really* like him."

I let her spin me a few times. It feels like the dances we used to do as guppies. Those were days of pure joy, before pressures or responsibilities or *boys*. Life was so much easier.

"It doesn't matter," I say. "Because he said he can't like me back."

"That's what he thinks."

"Oh no," I say. "Don't you get that determined look on your face."

"Leave things to me," she says. "I'll make sure he sees exactly what he's missing."

The hairs on the back of my neck stand on tiptoe. "Don't you dare."

"It'll be perfect." Her eyes go all dreamy, like she's already planning the wedding.

"Lily Sanderson," I warn, and when she doesn't respond, I get serious. "Princess Waterlily."

"What?" she asks with a long-suffering eye roll.

"Promise me." I get in her face, making sure she's looking me straight in the eye. "Promise me you won't do anything. At all. Nothing involving me and Riatus."

After last night's humiliation, the last thing I want is to see him. Ever.

"Involving you *and* Riatus?" she muses. "Okay. I promise. Nothing."

"Lily . . ."

"You worry too much," she says. "Now, let's go see what Laver has cooked up in the kitchens tonight. I hear there's pineapple inside-out cake."

One of the royal chef's specialties.

She takes me by the hand and swims for the door. I have a bad feeling about that promise. A really bad feeling.

The light is still on in Mom's studio when I get home. It's late and she's usually in bed by now. But with the Sea Harvest Dance less than two weeks away, she's swamped with orders and working crazy hours to make sure all the dresses are perfect.

Part of me misses being her apprentice. But I know she's really happy that I'm working with Lily. And I still help out whenever I have free time.

If only I had more time now.

When I swim through her door, she has a mouthful of pins and she's busy draping a swath of opulent lavender satin on a dress form. As I float there watching, she pins and repins it four times, finally settling on a fitted bodice with a fan of pleats across the chest. It's a work of origami art.

"It's beautiful, Mom."

She twirls and smiles at me through the pins. "Hank hoo."

Luckily I can translate pin speak. "You're welcome."

I grab the magnetic bowl of pins from her worktable and hold it out for her. She removes the pins from her mouth and sets them inside.

"Is this the one for Venus?" I ask, guessing that the lavender will look breathtaking against her dark skin and black hair.

She nods. "I had to talk her into it. But she'll see."

They always do.

"How many do you have left?" I ask.

A dozen dress forms are scattered around the room, covered in various stages of dressmaking. A few only have seam-line markings traced onto the cloth surface. Several display gowns are all but finished, just needing one last piece of decoration or a final hem. The bulk of them are somewhere in between, with fabric or trim pinned on, fittings and finishings still to come.

"Besides the ones on the forms," she says, turning to look at the piles of cloth on her worktable, "a dozen more."

"A dozen?" I gasp. "Mom, how will you finish them all?"

She shrugs. "I always find a way."

"I wish you would hire a new apprentice." And not just because that would relieve some of my guilt.

"I will." She picks up a spool of ribbon, one shade darker than the lavender satin, and holds it up against the dress-in-progress. "As soon as I find a candidate with the promise and the passion."

In other words, never. No one ever lives up to Mom's standards.

"Can I at least do something to help?"

I expect her to say no, because she always does. She doesn't want to take away from my fledgling career in politics. She's always wanted something more for me.

So it's a total shock when she says, "Actually, you could do one thing."

"Anything," I say with a smile.

"I'm running low on pearls," she says, and my stomach turns inside out. "Could you run to Paru's stall for me tomorrow?"

Mom's back is to me, so she can't see the look of pure horror that I'm sure is on my face right now. Really? Of all the things, all the trimmings she might need or all the tasks she could ask me to do, it's this?

I have to do something about this luck of mine.

"Sure," I say, trying not to sound like it's the end of the word. "How many do you need?"

"Two thousand should get me through this season. I'll leave a list on the kitchen counter." She throws a grateful smile over her shoulder. "Thank you, sweetheart."

I smile back, but mine's not nearly as cheery.

"No problem."

Yeah, no problem at all.

FIVE

The fact that it's daylight this time as I approach the stall in the back corner of the market only makes it feel like there's a spotlight on my humiliation. Oh look, there goes the mergirl who chased that hot merboy out of town, only to find out he couldn't like her.

Yeah, something like that.

Maybe he won't be there. Maybe he's not working the stall and I will find Coral waiting for me instead.

But as I round the corner, past the shellfish stall with the counter I hid behind the other night, now full of clams and oysters and every possible bivalve in the seven seas, the first thing I see is a flash of red. The vibrant scarf he uses to keep his hair out of his face is visible from a league away.

Way to keep up the winning streak, luck.

My mission is simple: get in, get the pearls, and get out. As fast—and as humiliation-free—as possible.

If my luck doesn't cooperate this time I'm going to make a visit to the Trigonum Vortex—what the human knows as the Bermuda Triangle—so I can make it disappear altogether.

There are several other customers swimming around the stall. That's a good sign. With so many other merfolk around, it can't become some kind of crazy scene. Of course that means there are more potential witnesses to my future humiliation, but I'm going to try thinking positive. It can't make things worse.

Riatus is helping another customer sift through a display of mint-green pearls.

"My Maggie loves seafoam green," the older mergentleman says. "I want to find the perfect one for our anniversary."

Riatus peers down at the pearls, inspecting them closely like it's just as important to him to find the right pearl. Finally, he plucks one out. "This looks like seafoam to me, sir. I'll bet your Maggie will adore this."

The customer beams, clearly pleased with the selection.

I enter on the other side of the stall and head for the cash register at the counter. They'll be over here in a moment so the gentleman can pay, and then I can intercept Riatus before he gets involved with another customer. I don't want to draw out this visit any longer than I have to.

"Normally a pearl like that runs fifty starbucks," he tells the gentleman as they approach the counter. "But today is your lucky day. We're running a discount on all green pearls. It's a bargain for twenty."

I grumble to myself. Riatus knows how to be charming when he wants to be.

Not waiting to see the gentleman's face, Riatus turns to swim around the counter . . . and sees me waiting there.

"Peri." He obviously didn't expect to see me back here anytime soon.

You and me both.

"I need to pick up a selection for my mom," I explain, so he doesn't get the wrong idea and think I'm here to beg him to date me, or something equally stupid.

"Right." He shakes his head, like he has to remind himself to be professional. "I'll help you as soon as I get Mr. Zafra checked out."

I cross my arms and float against the counter, determined not to notice how kind he's being to the elderly man. Or how the silver shells in his hair sparkle in the filtered sunlight. Or how his smile—and the shallow dimples in his cheeks—seem totally genuine. I am not interested in noticing anything worth admiring.

When Mr. Zafra has paid and swum off, another customer approaches Riatus. He puts her off. "Just let me help Peri," he tells her. "Her order will only take a moment."

The woman nods and goes back to browsing.

When Riatus turns back to face me, his cheeks are slightly pink and he doesn't quite look me in the eye. "How many does your mom need?"

"Two thousand."

"What colors?"

I hand him the list Mom wrote up. He gets to work, gathering a hundred in one shade, three hundred in another. I keep my eyes on the stall floor.

He swims back over and waves the list in front of my face.

"What does that last item say?" he asks. "I can't make it out."

I glance at the paper. Now it's my turn to blush. "Copper. Fifty copper seed pearls."

Which is not actually what the note says. Mom wrote *Fifty Peri seed.* Those must be for my dress, copper to match my tail fin. She's been very secretive about the design.

A moment later, Riatus has the whole order collected and bagged. I join him at the cash register.

"You got home okay the other night?"

The question completely throws me off my guard. I'm trying to keep this professional—nothing but business, like the incident at the edge of the forest never happened. He can't ask me about that night. He just can't.

"Yes," I answer.

"Good," he says. "I was worried about you."

Even though his attention is focused on totaling up the order, I shrug in response. I don't care if he doesn't see it.

He starts to punch numbers into the register. "I wanted to apologize."

"There's nothing to apologize for."

"I think there is." He looks up. "I wish I could—"

"Excuse me," a male customer asks, swimming up next to me. "Miss, may I borrow your opinion?"

"Mine?" I gesture at my chest.

"I need some advice."

He holds up two strands of classic white pearls. The strand in his left hand is made up of large-diameter pearls, more valuable and ostentatious than the other, smaller-diameter strand. Most mermen would go for the bigger pearls—the bigger, the better. But there is something to be said for understated elegance.

"Personally," I reply, "I would choose the more delicate strand."

His face scrunches up like he's surprised by my response. "Not what I expected," he say. "But you are obviously a mergirl of impeccable taste."

He winks at me and then swims off to put the larger strand back.

When I turn back to the register, Riatus looks annoyed. What did I do?

Then I realize he's not looking at me; he's looking at the other customer. Okay, what did *he* do? You know what, I don't even care. I just want to get out of here before my luck flows south again.

"What's my total?"

He ignores the cash register. "Peri, we need to talk."

I don't think so. He did plenty of talking the other night. I'm pretty much all talked out right now.

"Sorry," I say, even though I'm not. "I'm in a hurry."

He scowls. "It will only take a minute."

"No matter how much I might want to"—how does he like hearing those words?— "right now I just can't."

His jaw muscles tighten and his gaze intensifies. Clearly he didn't enjoy getting his own words thrown back at him. Too bad.

I'm done playing doormat Peri.

"You know what?" I say, grabbing the bag of pearls off the counter. "Send my mother the bill."

With a flourish of current, I spin away and sweep out of the stall. Score one for good luck. Finally.

"Mom, I've got the pearls," I shout into the house when I get home.

"She's not here," Lily says. "She had to go do an on-site fitting for Astria."

I whirl around to see my best friend floating in the doorway to the kitchen.

"That is so typical," I complain. "Astria knows my mom is swamped getting ready for the dance. She shouldn't have to make house calls so late in the process."

"I know, right?"

Lily has a weird smile on her face, like it's spread a little too wide to be natural. My spine stiffens. Lily only gets that weird smile on her face if she's up to something. And judging from the way her eyes are widening as I study her, I think she's definitely planning something that she knows I won't like.

"What's going on?" I ask cautiously as I swim toward her.

"I didn't find any baggies," an unfamiliar male voice says, "so I used a kitchen towel to hold the ice."

I scowl at Lily. What is going on here?

A merman—a merboy, really—floats up behind Lily, with one of our kitchen towels—apparently full of ice—held against his forehead. He looks about eighteen, with blond hair, a lopsided smile, and thick, black-framed glasses.

"That's great, Lom," Lily says, not breaking eye contact with me. "Peri, this is Lomanotus. He works for my dad. He's an intern. Lom, this is my best friend, Periwinkle Wentletrap."

He swims forward and offers me his free hand—the other still holding the ice pack in place. "Nice to meet you, Miss Wentletrap."

Everything about him is formal. His short blond hair is perfectly groomed. He's wearing a shirt and tie. When I take his hand, he shakes mine like I'm a new business acquaintance.

And, oh yeah, he called me *Miss Wentletrap*. No one under the age of sixty calls me Miss Wentletrap. It's Peri or, at most, Periwinkle. Who is this guy?

"Um, sure," I say, frowning at Lily as subtly as I can without being rude. "Nice to meet you too."

His smile lops to the other side and my stomach sinks. I have a feeling I know exactly what he's doing here.

"Lily, can I, um"—I give her an emphatic look—"see you in the kitchen for a second?"

"Okay," she says as I grab her hand and drag her after me at full force. She calls out over her shoulder, "We'll be right back."

The moment we're out of earshot, I demand, "What are you doing?"

"Helping Lom find an ice pack," she replies, as if she doesn't know what I'm really asking. "He hit his head on the doorframe."

"Lily . . ."

"Funny story, actually." She looks around the room, at the ceiling, the counters—anywhere but at me. "Apparently he's really clumsy when he's nervous."

"Lily . . ."

"And apparently," she continues, "he's nervous *a lot*."

"Lily!"

She stops and looks me in the eye.

I kick forward and whisper, "Why is there boy with an ice pack and a pocket protector in my front hall? What are you planning?"

"Nothing," she says, giving me that innocent smile.

"You need to reexamine your definition of nothing." I gesture toward the front entryway. "Why did you bring a boy to my house?"

She shakes her head, like she's going to deny what we both know she's doing. But then she must realize that I know her better than anyone and she can't pull one over on me.

"I just thought," she says, "that if Riatus is being such a jerk, you might be better off looking for someone else."

My eyes narrow. That sounds like too simple of an answer.

"No," I say. "You love that I have a crush on a bad boy who looks like a pirate. You think he and Quince will be besties and we can go on double dates." I jam my hands on my hips. "What are you *really* doing?"

She drops her head to one side and sighs. "Fine, smarty-pants. I thought it would do you both—you and Riatus—some good for him to see you as . . . desirable."

"Desirable?"

"As in, desired by other mermen." She stares at me, waiting for me to get it, but I don't. Finally, she gives. "You should make him jealous."

"Jealous?" I laugh out loud. "Lily, he doesn't like me. You can't make someone jealous if they don't like you."

"You said he *can't* like you," she argues, "not that he doesn't. And I'm pretty sure you can. If you go out with Lom—let Riatus see you out with Lom—then maybe that will make him think twice about why he *can't* go out with you."

I can't believe this is the crazy scheme my best friend has cooked up. Sure, she has a point that Riatus never said he didn't like me, just that he can't, but is there really a difference? The end result is the same: my feelings remain unrequited.

"I can't believe you thought this would work." I drop my voice to a furious whisper. "I can't believe you involved that poor boy in this ridiculous plan."

"He doesn't know anything about the plan," she insists. "He just thinks I'm setting you two up on a date."

"That makes it worse," I say with a sigh. "You're only messing with my love life because Quince is on the mainland visiting his mom."

"That's not true."

I cross my arms and raise my brows.

"Okay, maybe it's a little bit true," she relents. "I just want you to be happy. Quince is hoping to be back in time for the dance. If I get to go with the boy of my dreams, you should too."

When she puts it like that, I almost want to let her try.

She means well. She's so ecstatically happy with Quince, I know she just wants to help me find that same happiness. But sometimes her plans are a little misguided.

"I don't want to play any games," I say. "If he doesn't like me—" When Lily opens her mouth to argue, I correct, "If he *can't* like me, then he can't like me."

"Fine," she says. "I shouldn't have interfered."

"I know you're just trying to help, but this is something I have to figure out on my own."

"Understood." She grins at me. "You should still go out with Lom. He's a sweetie, and you two have a lot in common."

I give her a wry smile. "Not today."

She nods before turning and swimming out of the kitchen. "Come on, Lom. Time to go."

"Nice to meet you," he says, his voice carrying through the house as Lily drags him to the door.

Make Riatus jealous? What a ridiculous idea.

I can't fall asleep. My mind keeps going over everything that has happened in the past few days. From following Riatus to the edge of the kingdom to seeing him at the market today, and then Lily bringing a nerdy merboy to my house.

I should be able to relax knowing that everything is settled. That I might as well give up on my crush on Riatus because that's all it will ever be, and that Lily won't try any more crazy schemes to make him jealous. I hope.

But my mind won't let it go.

There is an old mer saying that goes, *If you fall off the sea horse, you have to get right back on and try again.* That might be just the advice I need to get past this thing about Riatus.

If he is the sea horse I fell off of, then maybe I need to try another sea horse. Okay, that analogy went really bad very quickly, but the general meaning is sound. I need to go on a date. Not to make Riatus jealous—if that was even possible—but for me.

I mean, there's nothing wrong with Lom. In fact, beneath that nerdy exterior is . . . well, a nerdy interior, but he was sweet. Nerdy can be adorable sometimes.

And Lily did say we have things in common.

She had the motive wrong, but maybe she had the right idea.

I flip out of bed and kick over to my desk. I pull out my old bubble machine, the one Lily and I used to use to send messages back and forth between my bedroom and hers when we were little. I scribble a quick message to Lily on a little sheet of stationery.

I need to move on. Do you think Lom still wants to go out?

A few seconds later, I've popped the message into the pale blue bubble and I'm shooting it across the open water toward the palace.

This could be some kind of stupid rebound reaction. Or it could be exactly what I need to get over Riatus.

A few minutes later, a bright pink bubble floats in my window and lands on the center of my bed. I swim over, pop it, and pull out the message inside.

Of course he does! I'll talk to him tomorrow.

Okay, the plan is in action. Now I just need to get my mind—and my heart—to follow through.

SIX

I don't know why I set up this date. I don't know why I ever possibly even considered that this might be a good idea.

But I did and now, in less than two minutes, Lom is going to show up at my door and take me out. On a date.

Some people might think it's pathetic that after more than seventeen years of life under the ocean, I've never gone out with a boy before, and maybe it is. It's not that I haven't had offers before. A few merboys have asked me out over the years, but I never really wanted to say yes. When your parents had a true love match and you can see what that's really like—when you see your mom still loyal to him even years after he's gone—then that makes your standards really high, I guess.

And then there's the little matter of being in love—or believing myself to be in love—with Riatus since forever. What ordinary merboy stands a chance against a pirate?

The fact that I am now, at seventeen, about to go on my first date isn't all that awful. The horrible part is that I still wish I were going with someone else.

"It's wrong," I say to Lily. "I'm using him. It's not fair."

"It's one date, Peri." She fusses with my hair. "Not a bonding ceremony. You're allowed to go on a date."

"I guess, but it still feels—"

Ding, gong, ding.

My eyes widen. "He's here."

"Relax," Lily says, swimming to the door. "Just have a good time. Don't think of it as a *date*."

"Then what?"

"I don't know." She grins as she grabs the handle. "A *not* date."

I frown at her.

My heart is racing as she opens the door and lets Lom inside. He is wearing—I am not joking—a suit jacket and a tie. I glance down at the fluttery top Lily helped me pick out. I look like I'm going on a picnic. He looks like he's going to the opera.

Oh yeah, totally a *not* date.

If I were the kind of mergirl who went for nerdy cute, he would probably be my type.

"You look very pretty, Miss Wentletrap," he says, his head bowed a little.

"You look, um, nice too, Lom. And please"—I give Lily a this-is-so-wrong look—"call me Peri."

It's a good thing Mom is busy in her studio. She would find this absolutely hilarious. Or horrifying. Either way, I just want to get out of here and get this over with.

"Come on, Lom," I say, grabbing his arm and swimming for the door. "Let's go."

"Bye," Lily calls after us. "You kids have fun."

I throw one last angry-worried look over my shoulder and see Lily waving at me with a dreamy look on her face. She thinks this is so romantic. I think it's going to be a nightmare.

"I have our date all planned," Lom says, seemingly oblivious to the fact that I'm dragging him away from my house at breakneck speed.

See, *he's* thinking of it as a date.

"Oh yeah?" I ask absently.

Lily promised she would tell Lom this was just a casual thing. So he wouldn't think this was anything more than new friends hanging out.

She and I are going to have a serious conversation about promises and meddling in other mergirls' personal lives.

"It's a perfect plan," he says. "But it's a secret. You'll have to wait and see."

"Great," I say, because I think I have to.

But as we swim toward downtown, the rock in the pit of my stomach gets heavier and heavier. It's obvious that Lom is really excited and he's just going to end up getting his feelings hurt. But he seems like a nice guy and, who knows, maybe I'll have fun. I need to stop being so worried about this and just have a good time.

"The first stop," he says, "is the Thalassinian Marketplace. Have you ever been?"

The rock in my stomach turns into a boulder.

"Yeah," I reply. "I've been."

"It's one of my favorite places in the kingdom," he says. "Do you have a favorite stall?"

I used to. But now even the thought of going near Paru's Pearls makes me nauseous. What was I thinking going out on this date? Clearly I am emotionally imbalanced.

"No," I say, "I like them all."

"Well, I do," Lom says. "And that will be our final stop at the end of the tour."

I force a smile. "Sounds good."

I can do this. I can be just a girl out on a date having fun. I don't have to be tied up in knots about some complicated boy who doesn't know what he wants or doesn't want. I can swim through the market without freaking out. Besides, we might not even go anywhere near his stall. It is a really big market, after all.

It turns out that Lom and I do have a lot in common—more than Lily knew. We both love kelpberry cakes. We both think tentacles are the most disgusting things in the sea. And we are both interested in the law, although he will probably go directly to law school after his internship with the king, and I'm content to work on the diplomatic side for a while.

The only problem is that after two hours of floating around the market, tasting samples and window-shopping, I know we'll never be more than friends. It's not that I don't like him—I just don't like him *that way*. Mom always says she knew Dad was the one from the first moment she saw him. I know just as surely that Lom isn't the one.

Besides, as much as I want to say I'm done with Riatus, that I'm over him and I'll never think of him again, I know that's not true.

Some part of me—probably a larger part than I want to admit—is still hung up on him.

As Lom and I drift away from the stall full of giant conch shells, I know I need to tell him that there's no romantic future for us.

"Hey, Lom," I say as we swim down the aisle, "I'm having a really good time."

He turns and smiles so big that his cheeks push his glasses up. "Me too."

"I think you should know—"

"Hey, we're down to the last stop on my itinerary." He takes my hand and starts swimming faster. "It's my favorite stall in the whole market."

I have to start kicking just to keep up. He seems really excited, which makes it all the more urgent I tell him.

"Listen, Lom—"

"It's just down this aisle," he says. "And I'm going to buy you a souvenir from our first date."

Oh no. That's exactly what I'm worried about. That he thinks this is a first date, not an only date. Not a hanging-out-with-a-new-friend thing.

But as I open my mouth to tell him, he turns to face me and says, "I hope you like pearls."

My mouth snaps shut.

Oh no. Worst idea ever. Worst. Idea. *Ever.*

I should say something. I should tell him I hate pearls or I'm allergic or my obsessive ex-boyfriend works the stall. I should say *something*.

But my tongue is frozen to the roof of my mouth and I let Lom lead us toward doom.

I'm tempted to close my eyes. Maybe if I imagine I'm some-where else, some previously unknown mermaid magic will pop me there.

Unfortunately, the first thing that comes to mind is the Black Kelpforest, and there is no way I want to end up there again—even if it means discovering some new magical power. So my eyes pop open and I brace myself.

I scan the stall, looking for the telltale scarf and black hair. I don't see it.

Riatus isn't there.

But Coral is.

Her dark curls bounce as she swims over. "Peri," she cries, pull-ing me into a tight hug. "It's been a few days."

"Hi, Coral," Lom says from behind me.

"Lom?" She releases me and gives me a questioning look. "Do you two know each other?"

"We do now," he says. "It's our first date."

Coral's jaw drops. "Date?"

I shake my head, but Lom speaks before I have a chance to say anything, to explain anything.

"The princess set us up." He gives me a toothy grin and I have to fight the urge to roll my eyes.

Coral glances from me to Lom and back again. She might be young, but she's not stupid. I can see in her eyes—a familiar pale gray—that she understands exactly what's going on here. I start to give her a pleading look, but then I stop myself. What do I have to explain? What do I have to apologize for? Riatus pushed me away, not the other way around.

As if she can totally hear my internal monologue, Coral nods sagely. "Okay, then. Well, let me know if you need anything."

She winks at me—just like her brother. Then, with a flick of her tail fin, she's sailing across the stall to greet another customer.

"Come on," Lom says, pulling me toward a display of exotic black pearls. "Help me choose."

I float over to the barrel and study the contents. I need to tell Lom this will be our only date, but he seems to be having such a good time. Maybe I should wait until it's over. That's probably the nice thing to do.

The pearls in this barrel are so dark and shiny and beautiful that I can't help digging my hand into them.

"Do you have pierced ears?" Lom asks. "I was thinking a pair for you and one for me."

He chooses a large pearl and holds it up to his left earlobe.

"I'm going to get it pierced as soon as my internship is over."

I giggle at the thought of Lom with a black pearl stud in his ear. It's so different than his clean-cut, nerdy merboy look. Thick, black glasses and a black pearl stud. On some guys the stud would look tough. If Riatus had one it would give him even more of an edge, like he's daring anyone to say something about the girly pearl in his ear.

On Lom it just looks adorable.

"I think it's a great idea," I say, reaching forward to nudge the pearl down his ear to a better position. "You definitely should."

A shadow passes over us, blocking out some of the light from behind. Lom looks over my shoulder and smiles.

He holds up the pearl. "How much is this one?"

I expect Coral to answer.

When the voice is male, my spine stiffens.

"Fifty."

I sense movement and a second later Riatus is floating next to us. At first I'm frozen, stunned to see him after thinking he wasn't here. But then I see the intimidating look on his face. He's scowling at Lom, like he wants to take him out behind the market and beat the carp out of him.

Where does he get off?

I float closer to Lom's side and paste a thrilled smile on my face.

Grabbing a pair of black pearls from the bin, I hold them up to my lobes. "How much for a pair?"

Riatus's eyes narrow.

"For those?" His mouth kicks up to one side. "Eighty-five."

"That's not bad," Lom says.

Riatus adds, "Each."

Lom's face falls. "Oh."

I drop the pearls back into the barrel. "That's okay," I say, my eyes focused on Riatus. "I'm kind of over pearls anyway."

"Yeah," Lom says, adding his to the pile. "Me too."

He seems completely oblivious to the tension hanging in the water between me and Riatus. He's a sweet guy, but definitely clueless.

Riatus floats closer to me. "Oh really?"

"Yes." I lift my chin. "Pearls are just too . . . complicated for me."

His pale gaze dips to my collarbone and then back up. "Are they?"

The urge to reach up and cover the copper pearl pendant hanging beneath my throat is almost overwhelming. But I resist. I won't give him the satisfaction.

I want to turn the tables.

Reaching up behind my neck, I start to unhook the chain. Riatus's hand is around my wrist before I can even locate the clasp.

"Don't." His voice is low and urgent.

I suck in a breath. His jaw muscles twitch and his eyes spear into mine. A moment passes between us, but for the life of me I can't figure out what it is.

Like I said, complicated.

"Do you two know each other?" Lom asks.

"No," I say.

At the same time, Riatus says, "Yes."

I wrench my wrist out of his grip. "I've been buying pearls here for years."

The tension in the water snaps, like the spark of an electric eel. Lom drifts backward a little. Riatus's demeanor shifts and warning bells chime in my mind.

"Caught her stealing once," he says with a smirk. "Would have turned her over to the police if she hadn't begged so prettily."

I slap him. Hard. My hand just lashes out without a second thought.

Lom gasps.

Riatus doesn't jerk back or reach for his cheek. His eyes don't even waver from mine. It takes me a moment to realize he wanted to get a rise out of me. He was goading me and I stepped right into his trap. Maybe he didn't expect me to hit him, but he was trying to make me mad.

Well, I don't like being manipulated.

Scowling, I grab Lom's wrist and swim away. I won't even dignify Riatus's behavior with a response. And I ignore the feel of his eyes on me until we're out of sight.

SEVEN

Usually King Whelk presides over all royal affairs. But when he's out of the kingdom—like this week, when he's attending a pan-kingdom summit in the South Pacific—Lily takes over his role in overseeing audiences with the crown. She spends the whole day—at least until there are no more citizens seeking an audience—listening to complaints and mitigating minor disputes.

Thalassinia doesn't have a court system like they do on the mainland. The crown hears grievances, confers with advisors and other experts if necessary, and makes the final rulings. Only the largest disputes require the entire royal council to get involved. For most things, arbitration by the king or crown princess satisfies all parties involved.

Lily is getting better with every session.

As her emissary, it's my job to have information about any relevant laws or statutes on hand to help her make her decisions.

Since most of the audiences are about minor squabbles, I'm usually on standby. It gets pretty boring—for both of us—and by the end we've often deteriorated into silliness.

Not today.

Our first hearing is a dispute between a pair of sea-slug farmers about the upcoming races at the Sea Harvest Festival.

"Every year!" Mr. Moorella shouts. "Every year, *he* cheats and wins the sea-slug race."

Mr. Phidian scoffs. "I do *not* cheat."

"Then explain it to me," Mr. Moorella barks. "How do your slugs come in first at the festival *every year?*"

"My slugs are obviously faster," Mr. Phidian replies coolly.

Mr. Moorella dives for Mr. Phidian, and soon they're swinging and swishing, sending waves of water across the room. Mangrove, the king's royal secretary who coordinates and documents all court proceedings, dashes between them and pushes them apart.

"Gentlemen," he exclaims.

"Please," Lily says, swimming off the throne and down to the meet the farmers at ground level. "I'm sure we can find an agreeable solution."

She glances back over her shoulder at me and I nod. I grab the binder that contains all the relevant rules and regulations about the Sea Harvest Festival and start flipping through. When I get to the section about the slug races, I quickly skim over the official rules.

In the third paragraph down, I find something that might help.

"Are your slugs the same breed?" I ask, looking up from the binder.

"No," Mr. Phidian replies, smoothing down his jacket after the scuffle. "I raise dorids and Moorella breeds aeolids."

Aha! Two different branches of the sea-slug family.

"Well, according to the official race rules," I say, reading from the relevant code, "if there are sufficient entrants so as to require more than one race, the races may be divided by nudibranch infraorder."

Lily blinks at me. "Say what?"

"It means," I say, slamming the binder shut, "we can run *two* races. One for dorids, and one for aeolids."

The two farmers glare at each other warily. Lily beams.

"Does that solve your dispute, gentlemen?" she asks.

Grumbling, they both agree. Moments later, Mangrove is escorting them from the room, soon to return with the next unhappy citizen.

Thinking about the festival makes me think about Riatus. Pretty much everything makes me think about him, but this relates to my current concerns.

"I am so seriously confused," I say. "Riatus is acting so weird."

"What happened?" she asks. "I thought you were giving up on him. How was your date with Lom?"

I twist in my seat—a small chair next to the throne—so that my tail fin drapes over the arm. "You want to know where he took me?" I hang my head back over the other arm. "To the market."

"No," Lily gasps.

I nod, sending my dark hair swirling around me. "And guess *where* in the market."

"No!"

"Yes," I exclaim. "He wanted to buy me pearls."

"No!"

There is something less-than-surprised about her tone.

"Did you have something to do with that?" I demand. "Did you tell him to take me to Paru's stall in some misguided—against-my-wishes—attempt to make Riatus jealous?"

"Of course not," she insists. "That was all his idea."

I glare at her.

Mangrove returns to the throne room and announces the next audience.

Lily waves them forward. She doesn't need me for this one, so I stare at the ceiling and don't think about Riatus. The throne-room ceiling is a wonder—intricately carved designs that include all sorts of elements of sea life from beautiful butterflyfish to slimy squid, coral to sea fans, and everything in between. It's as if someone took all the ocean's life and wove it together in picturesque, breathtaking relief. There are even a few jellyfish, but I try to ignore them.

Just like I'm ignoring thoughts of Riatus.

Lily processes the complaint quickly and a few minutes later she's turning back to me.

"Was Riatus there?"

I sit up. "Yes."

"Did he say anything?"

Boy did he. "He was kind of a jerk."

Lily leans over the arm of the throne, her blond hair surrounding her like a halo. "Like, how?"

"Like . . . I don't know." I grab my own hair and start weaving it into a braid. "Just a jerk."

Mangrove announces another citizen, and this time Lily needs to know the relevant zoning laws about building above the city—as in *floating* above the city. Needless to say that it's pretty much forbidden, except in cases of temporary structures. No one wants some new building blocking out what little sun we get down here.

As soon as that discussion is settled, Lily swims out of her seat and spins in a circle. When she whirls back to face me, she has that up-to-something smile on her face.

"So I take it you won't be seeing Lom again?" Lily asks.

I roll my eyes. "He couldn't say good night fast enough after we left the market. Who can blame him after Riatus told him he caught me stealing pearls once?"

Lily's eyes narrow. "Did you tell him it wasn't true?"

"Yes." I fidget with the hem of my top.

"I thought Lom would be more understanding." She studies me. "What aren't you telling me?"

I swear, Lily can smell gossip from a mile away.

"Okay, maybe it was because I hit Riatus."

"You hit him?" Lily gasps.

"I slapped him. Hard." I shrug. "He deserved it."

"I'm sure he did."

Lily falls silent for a moment, and I'm not sure if I should be relieved or worried. At the same time, the memory of Riatus's attitude, of how he was trying—and succeeding—to make me mad, just makes me mad all over again.

"Riatis was jealous!" she blurts. Then, almost to herself, "I knew he would be."

"What? No." I shake my head. "He practically told me to take a swim."

Lily's smile only gets bigger. "Of course he was jealous. He couldn't just say so. He's a guy."

"I know, but . . ."

But what?

I'm saved from trying to examine the answer to that question by Mangrove announcing another visitor. We're swamped for the rest of the day with no time to argue about whether Riatus was or was not jealous—for the record: was not. By the time we're through, I'm exhausted and just ready to go home and crash.

Lily swims me to the front door. As I head out across the palace grounds, she shouts, "He was jealous!"

I shake my head. I don't have the energy to answer. With a quick wave back over my shoulder, I hurry for home.

I'm halfway there when I remember that we ran out of plumaria pudding last night. Plumaria pudding is my pity-party indulgence of choice and I try to make sure we're never out of stock.

I veer left and head for the nearest grocery store, which is only a few blocks from my house. I may not have the entire store layout memorized, but I know exactly where to find the plumaria pudding.

When my shopping basket is loaded with double my normal amount—it's been a crazy couple of weeks and I've been going through it faster than usual—I turn and head for the checkout.

Only I don't check behind me first, and I end up swimming into another body. My basket goes sailing, and tubs of pudding swirl off into the aisle.

"I'm so sorry," I blurt, diving for the nearest tub. "I was in a hurry and I—"

The guy I just crashed into looks up and I freeze. It's the military-jacket merman I saw in Paru's stall the first day Riatus was back. What was his name?

"Oh," I say brilliantly. "You're Riatus's friend."

He smiles as he hands me a pair of the float-away tubs. "Prax."

"I'm Peri." I stuff the tubs back into my basket.

Prax nods. "You must be the mysterious mergirl who has my friend so distracted lately."

"I am?" I blurt before I can control my reaction. "I mean, I'm not. We're . . . not even friends or anything."

"I'm glad to hear that." Lines crinkle at the corners of his eyes and mouth as he smiles, like he's really happy to learn that Riatus and I aren't . . . anything.

He chases after the last three tubs of pudding.

I hold out my basket so he can place them inside. "Why is that?"

"Because that means I can ask you out," he says with a wink.

I almost drop my basket again.

"You can?" Lord love a lobster, I sound like a moron. "I mean, you can. If you want to."

He drifts a little closer. "Oh, I want to."

The question is, do *I* want to?

That same odd feeling that tickled the back of my neck when I first saw him tickles my neck now. Something about him bothers me, but I can't put my tail fin on exactly what. Maybe I'm just being paranoid.

Plus, there's the part where he's Riatus's friend. Lily's insistence that Riatus was jealous over my date with Lom makes me wonder . . . Would he be *actually*—or, if Lily is right, *even more*—jealous if I went out with his friend? I guess there is only one way to find out.

"I would love to," I say before he even officially asks.

"Great." He floats a little closer. "How about tomorrow night? Sunken Treasure Pizza?"

I can already picture Riatus's face.

"Sounds perfect." I smile in anticipation. "It's a date."

Sunken Treasure has the best pizza in all of Thalassinia. Sal, the owner, originally hails from the Mediterranean kingdom of Posidonia, which stretches from the west coast of Italy to the gates of Gibraltar. And those merfolk know how to make an amazing pizza.

They are always swamped, even on an ordinary Tuesday night, so when I get there before Prax I have to wait a few minutes for a table. While I'm floating in the little alcove next to the hostess podium, the door opens. I look up, hoping it's Prax.

Instead, I see Riatus holding the door open for Coral. Oh no.

Luckily, he's facing the other way and I'm hidden in shadows. I drift back and watch as they swim up to the hostess.

"Welcome back, Riatus. Your regular table is all set," she says with a huge smile on her face. "Follow me."

Riatus lets Coral go first and then they disappear into the restaurant.

His regular table? He must come here a lot. Did Prax know that when he suggested we eat here? This was the worst idea ever—I'm just full of those lately. Why did I think that I wanted to make him jealous? I'm going to throw up.

"There she is," Prax says as he swims through the door.

I try not to look wild-eyed as I tell him, "This was a bad idea. We should go."

He scowls. "Why?"

"Riatus is here," I say. "This is going to be awkward. It already is."

"I thought you weren't even friends."

"We're not, it's just—" I have to get out of here. "It's complicated."

Prax's smile gentles and he swims to my side. "This isn't," he insists. "It's dinner. Nothing more. You're allowed to go to dinner, aren't you?"

"Of course I'm—" I stop short, smiling as I realize he was trying to talk me into a corner. "Oh, I see what you did there."

The hostess returns to the podium. "Your table is ready."

Prax holds out his arm. "Come on. I've been dying to try their calamari-and-kombu deep dish."

He's right. This is just dinner. And Riatus doesn't have a say in who I have dinner with. If he has a problem with this, then it's *his* problem. Not mine.

I take Prax's offered arm and we follow the hostess to our table. In my wildest fantasy, there would be a huge scene. I picture Riatus turning over tables and sending pizzas spinning through the water. A fight or an argument or at least an exchange of words.

Nothing like that happens.

So underwhelming.

He sees us. I know he sees us because the water temperature changes and, well, every time I look over at their table he's glaring at us. But he doesn't do or say anything. He finishes his meal with Coral and when they're done they leave, swimming right past our table on the way to the door.

Coral waves at me as she swims by, casting a worried glance at my dinner companion. Riatus nudges her forward. He doesn't even look at us.

When the door closes behind them I slump back into my seat.

"A little anticlimactic," Prax says. "Don't you think?"

I nod.

And more than a little disappointing. I've never been so sad to be proven right. Riatus wasn't jealous, but I'm not even looking forward to gloating about that to Lily.

Tomorrow, I'm putting all of this behind me. I'll never think of him again.

Prax offers to swim me home, but I want the night to be over. I want to get back to my house and curl up in my bed.

Only when I get there, I'm too wired to sleep. My body is full of restless energy. I can't even think of going to sleep yet.

Instead, I head for Mom's studio. Maybe I can get a little work done for her, or at least clean up.

Cleaning is always a great outlet for excess energy.

I start by putting away the trims-and-notions containers Mom has strung all over the room. Little bins of buttons and sequins, rolls of lace and piping, and several jars of pearls. As I'm placing the jar of tiny copper pearls back on the shelf—between the bronze ones and the chocolate-colored ones—I feel the telltale tingle in my eyes.

Of all the stupid things to cry about. Riatus never made any promises to me, never even asked me on an actual date or told me he likes me. Why would I even bother wasting tears on him?

And, more importantly, why can't I stop?

"Do you store everything in color order?"

I shriek.

For the space of time it takes my brain to recognize Riatus's voice, my scream echoes through the water. I smack my hand over my mouth as I spin around to face the window.

I hope that didn't wake Mom.

Riatus is floating just outside, looking like he wants to come in but is afraid to. His pale eyes practically glow against the darkness of his hair and the night sea beyond.

I race to the window, careful to keep my voice low.

"What are you doing here?" I demand. "How do you even know where I live?"

He shrugs. "I've been delivering pearls to your mom for years."

I open my mouth to argue—just for the sake of arguing—but then I realize how dumb that makes me look. Of course he's delivered pearls to our house. I used to watch him from my bedroom window.

But that doesn't answer my first question.

"That doesn't explain why you're here," I say. "Lurking outside my window in the middle of the night."

"It's not the middle of the night," he argues. "And it's not your window. It's the studio."

"But you *are* lurking."

He shrugs again, as if he's not going to argue.

I demand, "Why?"

He swims through the window and drifts to a stop mere inches from me. "To warn you. Prax is nothing but trouble."

My inner mergirl does a little dance of victory, even as I acknowledge that this means Lily was right. He *is* jealous!

"I don't see how it's any of your business," I throw back. "You can't even like me, remember?"

"Don't tempt me to make it my business," he warns.

I laugh in his face. Is it just me, or is this getting ridiculous?

"He's a great white," Riatus says. "You're just a guppy."

"I'm more than capable of taking care of myself." I turn away from him. "You weren't invited in."

His hand wraps around my upper arm and he spins me back to face him.

"I'm serious, Peri." His face is so close our noses are practically touching. "Stay away from him."

I lean back, trying to get enough distance to clear my thoughts.

"Or you'll what, Riatus?" I draw in a deep breath. "I don't belong to you."

His voice is almost sad as he replies, "I know."

My breath whooshes out of me in a swirl of current. We're breathing the same water. He's so close I can feel the heat radiating off his body, warming me even as chills race down my spine.

In that moment, for just the barest hint of a second, I think about what it would be like to give my tail fin a tiny flick and press my lips against his.

As soon as the thought floats into my mind, I swirl it right back out. It's wrong—so wrong on so many levels. In the human world, a kiss might be just a kiss, but down here . . . it's so much more. The magic of a mer bond isn't something to be entered into without the deepest of love. It's an almost sacred connection between a couple.

Even the *thought* of rushing that kind of bond makes me feel guilty.

Almost as if he senses my thoughts, his gaze drops to my mouth for an instant before looking away. We both know that's not the answer to the problems between us. It would only make things worse.

He turns and swims for the window, pausing before continuing through.

"Hate me if you want to," he says over his shoulder. "But don't use Prax to get my attention. You'll pay too high a price."

Then he's gone.

That's exactly my problem. I *can't* hate him, even if I want to. I'm just going to have to find a way to live with that.

EIGHT

"You look breathtaking."

Mom's eyes are sparkling with tears as I twirl in the dress she made me for the Sea Harvest Dance. The skirt swirls out around my tail fin, a circle of dreamy, ombré chiffon. A rich mahogany brown at the hem, the dress gradually lightens as it goes up. The bodice is a shimmery copper, covered in dozens of tiny copper pearls.

I feel like a mermaid princess.

"You will capture everyone's attention," Mom says.

She floats down to fuss with the hem. Never fully happy with a dress, she's always fixing this or tweaking that until the moment it swims out the door.

"I'm not looking for attention," I reply. "I just want to have a good time."

Mom looks up, a skeptical smile in place. "If you say so."

I smile back at her. It's been the two of us for so long that sometimes we feel more like sisters than mother and daughter. I talk to her about almost everything, but some things—like a certain confusing merboy—I keep to myself.

"Why are boys so complicated?" I ask. "Why can't they just, I don't know, be normal?"

Mom laughs as she floats back up from my hem. "If love weren't complicated," she says, "then what would be the fun?"

"I can think of a thousand things," I grumble.

"Are we talking about a specific merboy?" she asks. "I thought you were going to the dance with Lily."

"Maybe," I say, answering her first question as I grab my clutch from the table by the front door. "And I am going with Lily."

Mom swims forward and plays with the carefully pinned curls in my hair. She gets this dreamy look on her face that I always assume means she's thinking of Dad. He's been gone for years and she still misses him.

It's a testament to their love that she has never sought to sever their bond. In her mind they are still married.

"It will work out," she finally says, swimming back to admire my whole image. "These things always do."

The front door opens and Lily swims in, her royal escorts waiting outside. She's wearing the dress Mom made her, a bubbly froth of iridescent lime-green-and-gold tulle over silk. She looks like beautiful Caulerpa bouquet.

Quince wanted to be back in time to be her date to the festival, but she got a note this afternoon that he wouldn't make it. I'm bummed for her, but that's good news for me. At least I won't have to go alone.

"Are we going to knock 'em dead or what, Mrs. Wentletrap?" Lily says as she floats to my side.

Mom smiles and shakes her head, her eyes sparkling even more than before.

"Without a doubt." She presses her hands to her chest. "Someone needs to invent a sea camera so I can take a picture of this moment."

Lily throws me a sideways smile. "Well, it just so happens . . ."

She reaches into her tiny purse and pulls out a bright yellow plastic camera, one of those ones designed for underwater photography. We don't have the technology to develop film in the mer world, or the electricity to process digital pictures. Some things just don't translate into underwater life.

Lily hands her camera to Mom and then floats back to my side.

"I'll have the pictures printed next time I visit Aunt Rachel." She wraps an arm around my shoulder and hugs me tight. "I'll get a set printed on waterproof paper."

Mom beams. I hug Lily back and we pose for the camera.

"I'm sorry Quince couldn't make it," I whisper between shots.

"Me too," she replies with a wistful smile as she takes my hand. "But you're a pretty decent consolation date."

I grin and squeeze her hand.

By the time we swim off for the dance, Mom must have taken fifty pictures.

I just hope my good luck decides to hang out for a while so tonight is memorable in a good way.

The Sea Harvest Dance is the biggest underwater social event of the year, despite the terrible trio's attempts to make their birthday bashes even more spectacular. King Whelk turns the entire palace grounds over to the royal party planners for the event. Bioluminescent fairy lights dot every surface and every corner with a rainbow of glow, making it look like nightfall in a magical kingdom—which it kind of is. Reggae dance music floats all around. Dozens of tables are spread out with the finest delicacies our kingdom—and the entire mer world—has to offer.

It all centers around the huge dance floor laid out in the south garden: a one-hundred-foot square surrounded by the glittering swirl of an artificial whirlpool. Legend says that any couple who kisses on the dance floor will be forever happy.

It's just a romantic fairy tale, but it's fun to think about.

"Where should we start?" Lily asks. "Food, drink, or dancing?"

"What about the carnival?"

I can see the top of the torpedo tube poking up behind the palace. It's an amazing ride. A giant circular tube made of clear plastic, open at the bottom so merfolk can get in. Once inside, the three operators merge their powers to send the water inside the tube rushing, taking the riders with it. It's like being a launched torpedo.

Lily grins. "Let's do it."

She grabs my hand and we swim around back. One day we'll probably feel too old to ride the rides, but for now we're going to have our fun while we can.

Two hours later, we've ridden every ride. Twice. It helps when your date is the princess and everyone offers to let her cut in line. She usually declined, but she gave in on the Octowhirl when we wanted to go a third time.

By the time we float back toward the dance floor, I've declared this the best Sea Harvest Festival ever. I haven't had to see or deal with or even worry about any merboys. It's been nothing but fun, just the two of us.

I can tell, though, that Lily is missing Quince.

"When does he come home now?" I ask.

She gives me a lovelorn smile. "Monday, after he takes his mom to work at her new job."

"Two days." I smile back. "That's not long at all."

She shakes her head as she looks out over the dance floor. "Nope, I can handle two more days." Her gaze stops on something—someone—and her mouth drops open. "Oh no."

I know what I'm going to see before I follow the direction of her stare. There, at the far edge of the dance floor, is Riatus.

"How dare he show up here?" she demands. "After he flirted with you and promised to—"

"He didn't flirt with me," I say. "He didn't promise me anything."

I spin to face her and swim backward toward the dance floor. "You know what, I'm going to dance by myself."

Lily swims after me. "Oh no you're not."

There is something freeing about dancing with your best friend in front of the entire kingdom. I can't say I'm not thinking about boys at all—Riatus is only half a dance floor away—but I'm trying not to. Lily and I let loose, dancing however we want. Wild, crazy, spinning, kicking, and generally sending the water around us into a tailspin. We draw the amused attention of some of the other dancers, but for the most part we're in our own world.

Until someone taps me on the shoulder.

I stiffen, seriously expecting it to be Riatus because—well, because . . . *my luck*. As I spin around, I'm only slightly relieved to see that it's Prax.

Despite my intention to completely ignore Riatus's unexplained warning about him, something has seemed a little off with him from the beginning. Still, he's been nothing but nice to me, so I smile.

"You two look like you're having fun," he says, flicking a glance at Lily, who is still dancing like a crazy mergirl.

"We are," I reply.

"I don't want to break up this awesome twosome," he says, "but I was hoping for a dance."

I hesitate. Something in my gut tells me to listen to Riatus on this one. But then again, something even bigger from somewhere in the vicinity of my bruised ego tells me that nothing would bother Riatus more than seeing me dance with Prax.

I kick my hesitation to the side, take his offered hand, and say, "I'd love to."

He leads me a little ways deeper into the crowd, and a little closer to where Riatus is dancing with his sister. Maybe Prax wants to stick it to Riatus as much as I do. Works for me.

"I hope that big lug didn't scare you off the other night," he says as we start dancing.

"Who, Riatus?" Do we really have to talk about him? I shrug. "He has no effect on my life whatsoever."

The band transitions to a new song, a slower song, and before I can think Prax has his arms around my waist and is pulling me closer. I force myself to relax. It's just a dance.

"You're better than him," he says.

I smile, even though I'm cringing inside. "Than who?"

He gives me a wry look. "Pirate boy. He's bad news."

I don't say, "He said the same thing about you."

My gaze drifts to the merboy in question. As much as I want to believe that—not liking him would be so much easier if I really thought he was trouble—my gut says he's not. I mean, how bad can he be if he's escorting his younger sister to the Sea Harvest Dance?

I glance their way. She looks like she's having the time of her life. This could even be her first dance. She *should* be having a great time.

Riatus, on the other hand, is fuming.

I turn away before he catches me looking.

"Let's talk about something else," I say. Anything else.

"I'd love to," Prax says, his gaze trained back over my shoulder. "But I don't think that's possible."

Before I can ask what he means, I feel a tap on my shoulder.

"Mind if I cut in?"

Prax releases me and I float to his side. This is supposed to be where I make a joke, pretend to think Riatus means he wants to dance with Prax and not me. But I'm not feeling very funny right now. I'm tired. Tired of this back and forth, of not knowing where I stand or what he wants from me.

I'm tired of being the toy in the middle.

"Actually, I do mind," I say. "I'm having a lovely dance and you are not welcome."

As I turn away from him, I see his brows drop and his jaw muscles twitch. I'm sure the smirk on Prax's face isn't helping. His arms are back around my waist in an instant, and he pulls me even tighter against him.

I wiggle a little, trying to put some space between us, but he holds firm.

"I can't breathe." It's an exaggeration, but I'm starting to feel a little claustrophobic.

"This is perfect," Prax replies. "He's going apoplectic."

"Seriously," I whisper furiously. "Ease off."

He does the opposite, squeezing tighter as his hands drift down from my waist.

I stop playing nice and brace my palms against his shoulder. I push with all my strength, but he doesn't budge.

I'm about to resort to something underhanded—biting, maybe, or a tail fin to the tenders—when suddenly he's whirling me away from him.

He grins. "This is going to be good."

"I warned you," Riatus says, and at first I think he's talking to me. "I warned you to stay away from her. From both of them."

Riatus faces off with him, floating just inches apart. His hands are clenched into fists and he looks ready to tackle Prax.

The crowd around us inches away, leaving the three of us in an open circle. I see Lily swim up to the edge and give me a questioning look. As if I have any idea what's going on here.

Prax spreads his arms wide. "It's a free kingdom. A mergirl can dance with whoever she wants."

Riatus shrugs. "That's true. And I guess I'm free to tell her just what kind of guy you really are."

"Who's the one with a record?" Prax taunts.

"I'm sure you'll have one soon enough."

Prax is swinging before Riatus finishes his sentence. Riatus dodges right and the punch misses, swooshing through open water. Before Prax can recover, Riatus lands a solid hit to his jaw. Prax goes sailing, flipping end over end into the crowd.

When he rights himself, he says, "You'll regret that."

"You know what?" Riatus shakes out his hand. "I don't think I will."

The crowd parts and a pair of royal guards swim into the circle. I recognize them from the palace.

"What's the trouble here?" one asks.

Prax points at Riatus. "That jackfish just assaulted me." He holds both hands up in the air, like he is blameless in this situation. "Arrest him."

The guards start for Riatus. I move into their path.

"No, that's not what happened," I insist. "Prax swung first. Riatus was just defending himself."

One of the guards, Barney, looks sympathetic, like he wants to believe me but it's my word against Prax's. "I'm sorry, Miss Peri, but with an accusation like that we really need to take them both in."

"She's right," Lily says, swimming to my side. "I saw the whole thing."

Barney looks from Lily to Prax and then back to Lily. "Yes, Princess. But I'm afraid we'll still have to escort both young mermen from the dance."

She looks at me and I nod. That's better than them arresting either of them.

They head for Riatus, but as they reach him he shrugs them off. "I was leaving anyway."

I watch, helpless and confused, as he swims off over the crowd, motions to his sister, and they head for the palace gates.

I'm still shaking my head when Lily says, "What are you waiting for? Go after him."

I'm kicking away before she finishes.

NINE

"**What the clamshell** is going on?"

Riatus stops moving but doesn't turn back to face me. "Nothing."
He starts to move again, his sister at his side.

"No," I say, speeding up to swim around them and plant myself in their path. "Not nothing. I'm tired of whatever game we're playing. I'm tired of you stepping in to warn me or protect me or perform whatever misplaced act of chivalry you think you need to do, and then telling me to go take a swim."

"Peri, this isn't the—"

"Oh yes it is." I swim close enough so that we're practically nose to nose. "This is exactly the time. This is exactly the place. You've ruined my evening and I want to know why."

His eyes look unfocused, like he's trying not to see me.

Next to him, his sister shifts. "Ri, tell her."

"No," he insists.

"Fine," she says, transferring her attention to me. "I'll tell her."

I shake my head. "If he can't tell me himself, then I don't want to hear it."

She wraps her arms around his arm. "Tell her."

We're far enough away from the palace that we can't hear the music. The streets of Thalassinia are deserted because everyone is at the dance.

He floats, frozen for several seconds. I'm holding my breath because this feels like a turning point. Either he gets over his problem and tells me what's going on or . . . he doesn't. If it's the former, then we have a chance. Otherwise, this is the end of the road.

If he can't even trust me enough to share whatever is keeping us apart, then there's no hope.

He's silent too long. He's not going to tell me, and I'm going to have to be strong and swim away with my head held high. I'll have to finally give up this ridiculous fantasy that maybe, one day, if the stars align and the currents cooperate, we can actually be together.

My shoulders slump. This is it. I never really thought I'd give up on him, but I won't be like Lily, convincing myself I'm in love for three years with nothing in return. I won't play the fool.

He turns and starts swimming away. Coral looks back at me over her shoulder, the look on her face a clear indication that she doesn't agree with her brother's actions.

Her and me both.

The distance is growing and I'm either too stunned or too tired of chasing to go after him.

It's over.

Lily serves giant globs of plumaria pudding into two bowls and sets them on my kitchen counter. I pull one toward me and dig a spoon into the blobby goodness.

"Boys," I say before shoving a huge bite into my mouth.

Lily nods. "Boys."

But she doesn't mean it. She and Quince are perfect—like made-for-each-other perfect. Her boy troubles are behind her.

"I don't want to talk about it anymore," I announce. "I'm swearing off boys. For good."

Lily giggles and I know she doesn't believe me. But I swear, after the Riatus roller coaster I've been on the last few weeks, I'm pretty sure I've had enough boy drama to last a lifetime. I will just dedicate myself to a life of service to the crown. After all, when she becomes queen, Lily will need me more than ever. I have to be ready.

The doorbell rings. Mom is upstairs passed out in her bedroom. She never goes to the Sea Harvest Dance because she's too exhausted after making all the dresses for it. I don't have the energy to drag myself to the door.

"I'll get it," Lily says, sounding way too chipper for my grumpy taste.

I keep eating my pudding and trying not to let thoughts of that boy whose name I don't want to think enter my mind.

A moment later, Lily calls out, "Peri, I think you want to come see this."

I slump. I probably don't. Judging by the way my luck has been going, it's bad news. Definitely not worth the effort of swimming through the house.

But as I swim into the front hall, I have to agree with Lily.

Floating there in my front door is Riatus's sister. I definitely want to see this.

I lean through the doorway and follow her gaze. Only to find Riatus floating a few feet away.

I scowl.

"After what happened," Coral says, "I didn't think you'd open the door for him."

"You're right."

I start to float back inside, but she grabs my wrist.

"Please. I know you've given him lots of chances."

I snort at the ridiculous understatement.

"But give him just one more." She smiles a huge, hopeful smile. "For me?"

I sigh. She is very convincing. I throw another scowl his way.

"Fine." I narrow my eyes at her. "One more."

She claps and waves him closer. "I'll just wait inside," she says, swimming past me and pulling Lily in with her. "With the princess."

An instant later, they're shut inside and Riatus is swimming to my side.

I bite my lips to keep from saying anything. I've said enough for ten conversations already. It's his turn. If he wants to say something, he'll have to say it.

"I'm sorry."

For the first words out of his mouth, they're pretty good ones. I release the bite on my lips.

"Coral pointed out that I might have been acting like a jackfish."

"You have," I blurt, then quickly bite my lips.

Finally, he looks up and meets my eyes.

"Prax is a bottom-feeder."

"Yeah, I figured that out," I say, "when he tried to grope me on the dance floor and have you arrested."

Riatus twists his head to crack his neck. "We used to be friends, for years. Before I . . . left. At least I *thought* we were friends."

"What happened?"

Riatus runs a hand back over his hair. He looks frustrated, like he's still struggling with the idea of telling me what's going on.

"Whatever it is," I say, "you can trust me."

He looks up, his eyes intense. "I know."

"Then tell me."

He closes his eyes, and when he opens them I can see he's ready.

"He's always been one of those guys who likes skirting trouble," Riatus begins. "Being just outside the problem when the wave hits the shore. At first, I was amazed he wanted to be my friend. He is a couple years older and, I thought, so much cooler."

It's on the tip of my tongue to tell Riatus that's ridiculous—I can't imagine anyone cooler than *him*—but I don't. This is not the right moment.

"At first I just wanted to please him. I did whatever he asked. Little things, like covering for him at school or lending him lunch money. Graffiti on the palace walls. Staying out all night, swimming the streets." He looks pained at the memory. "The older we got, the more serious . . ." He trails off, shaking his head. "One day, a little over a year ago, he decided to escalate to robbery. He told me the house was abandoned."

Even though the answer is obvious, I ask, "It wasn't?"

He shakes his head. "The police came. Prax slipped out the back."

"And you got in trouble?"

Dark hair swirls around him as he nods.

"Sounds like a real starfish," I mutter.

"Getting arrested was a wakeup call." He rolls his shoulders, trying to relieve some of the tension.

"You—" I begin, but as the words form, the puzzle pieces fall into place. "You didn't spend the last year on some grand adventure, did you?"

"No." He shakes his head. "I was a guest of the Thalassinian Juvenile Detention Facility."

I suck in a deep draw of breath. Now it all makes sense. Why he disappeared so suddenly. Why he seemed so much more mature—more serious—when he came back.

"Since I got out, I'm doing everything I can to avoid getting in trouble. I can't make my mom and Coral go through that again." His gaze lifts and there is so much pain in his eyes, I want to hug him. "That included avoiding Prax."

"Bet he didn't love that plan," I say. "Guys like that don't like being rejected—as I learned on the dance floor tonight. If you hadn't stepped in . . ."

"It was nothing," he says with a shrug.

I swim a little closer. "It wasn't."

He looks uncomfortable.

"Just say you're welcome," I tell him.

His mouth lifts up in a half smile. "You're welcome."

I beam. "Now, please continue."

Some of the tension leaves his shoulders.

"A few weeks ago, right after that first day I saw you in the market, Prax started flirting with my sister." His fists clench. "She's too young to see him for the trouble he is."

I imagine the worst. "He didn't hurt her?"

He shakes his head. "He's not interested in her. Not in that way. He only used her to get to me."

"I don't understand."

"Ever since I got back and refused to hang out with him, refused to be his easy get-out-of-jail-free card, he's been trying to get back at me." He takes a deep breath. "He finally found a way with Coral. He threatened to bond with her, just to spite me. To blackmail me."

"She's such a sweet girl," I say. How could anyone try to take advantage of her?

"She is," Riatus continues. "When I found a note asking her to meet him at the edge of the Kelpforest, I was ready to kill him."

Oh no! "That night I followed you?"

Riatus nods. "I was on my way to stop them."

And I stopped him. "They didn't. Did they?"

"Turns out Coral isn't as naïve as I thought," he says, shaking his head. "She knew it was bad news to meet a boy she didn't know in the most dangerous part of Thalassinia. She never planned to meet him."

"Smart girl." I swim forward and place my palms on his shoulders.

I look at Riatus—really, for the first time, *look* at him. I see the boy he was and the man he is working hard to become. He's full of guilt over his past mistakes and trying not to repeat them. His dad has been gone since forever, and he's shouldering the responsibility for his mom and sister. Protecting them.

Protecting me, too.

"So, tell me something," I say, letting my hands slide down his arms. "When you told me you *couldn't* like me . . . ?"

He looks down as I entwine my fingers through his.

"You thought you were shielding me? From Prax?"

Riatus doesn't look up, but his fingers tighten around mine. "He tried to use Coral against me. If he thought I even *might* have feelings for you, he would have tried to use you, too."

"Then why didn't you tell me the truth?" I dip down so I can meet his lowered gaze. "Why just give me vague warnings about Prax?"

"I *told* him to tell you," a voice calls out from inside the house. "You should have listened to me!"

"I know that *now*," he shouts back to his sister. He shares a conspiratorial look with me. "She has ears like sonar, I swear."

"I heard that!" she yells.

I grab him by the wrist and swim away from the house, out of even sonar earshot. I don't want any company for the rest of this conversation.

"She's right," I say softly when we're far enough away to be safe. "You should have told me."

"I didn't want you drawn into the situation." He tries to release my hands, but I don't let go. "Thanks to Prax—thanks to my own stupid mistakes—I've already hurt too many people I care about. I didn't want to hurt you, too."

"News flash," I say without sarcasm, "pushing me away hurts way more than anything Prax could do."

This time he manages to pull his hands away. I float closer, but he drifts back. As the space between us grows, I feel the progress we've made tonight slipping away.

"You're giving him all the power," I insist. "You're letting him and your past ruin whatever we might have together."

Riatus shakes his head, like he can't let go of this idea that he's protecting me by keeping me at a distance. If there's anything I've learned from seeing Lily and Quince, it's that two people are stronger together than they are individually.

It might take some convincing to make Riatus believe that, but I'm sick of dancing around the issue. Time to lay it all on the line. I close the distance. "I like you, Riatus. A lot."

His brow furrows in pain.

"Do you see this?" I sink down to meet his gaze as I gesture to the pearl hanging around my neck. When I'm sure he sees it, I say, "I told you it was a gift. Do you know who gave it to me?"

I fully expect him to say no because . . . well, why would he remember? It was *my* guppihood crush. To him I was just a little mergirl.

So I'm beyond stunned when he nods and says, "I did."

"You—?" I scowl. "You *remember*?"

His laugh is fierce and unexpected. "Of course I remember."

I smack him on the shoulder.

When his hand wraps around my wrist, holding my palm against his chest, I want to melt. There is something boyish about the small smile spreading across his lips.

"You were the sweetest girl," he says.

"Past tense?" I ask.

He looks up at me. "You still are. You were nice to Coral, even when she was annoying. And I—" His cheeks turn a little pink. "I knew you liked me."

The horrifyingly humiliated part of me wants to gasp, but the sincerity in his tone tells me I don't need to be embarrassed. Okay, I'm still a *little* horrified—who wouldn't be?

Looking me straight in the eye, he says, "I'm not good enough for you."

"You're right," I say, and I can tell he's stunned by my answer. "The way you've been acting, you *aren't*. But I'm willing to forgive and forget everything that happened since you came back, *if* you will answer one question."

"Okay," he agrees warily.

"Do you"—I sink down to meet his gaze—"like me?"

"What?"

"It's simple," I insist. "Do you like me or not?"

"Peri, I—"

"Yes or no, Riatus."

He winces like it will hurt to say the words.

"Yes. Or no." I repeat when he looks like he wants to argue again. "Yes or no. Yes or no. Yes or—"

"Yes!" he blurts. "Okay, yes."

"What was that?" I can't hide my smile.

"Yes," he admits, sounding relieved. His smile grows bigger until his dimples show. "I like you."

Finally!

"Was that so hard to say?"

He gives me an are-you-kidding look.

"You want to know a secret?"

"Sure."

"That's the only thing that matters," I say.

"What is?" He looks confused and I like it—it's about time those tables turned.

"I like you. You like me." I link my arm through his and swim back for the house. "In the beginning, that's all that matters."

His dark brows slash down, like he's not sure if he can believe me.

"It's a place to start," I explain as I push open the door, sending Lily and Coral scurrying out of the way. "Who knows where we go from here, but for tonight just liking each other is enough. Now"—I lead him toward the kitchen—"I have one more very important question to ask you."

"What's that?"

I release him and float over to the cabinet. "Do you like plumaria pudding?"

"Yeah," he says, jerking back in surprise. "It's my favorite."

I smile as I pull out another tub. Lily and Coral swim in to join us and soon we all have fresh bowls of pudding and life is good. Riatus and I can't stop smiling at each other. It's like admitting that we like each other opened some kind of floodgate.

Nothing in life is certain, but I know that with the whole truth out in the open we have a chance. We like each other, and that's enough for a perfect beginning.

⁕ ⁕ ⁕ ⁕ ⁕ ⁕ ⁕ ⁕ ⁕ ⁕

KEEP READING FOR TWO BONUS STORIES!

Periwinkle Wentletrap sailed into the Thalassinian Market-place with a smile on her face. Held once each month on the open sands of the old town square, the market boasted vendors of every kind hawking their wares. Farmers came from the rural regions, beyond the edges of the city, with barrels of sweet smelling sand strawberries, fresh kelp , and dried sea fans. Lobstermen put the fattest of their herd on display. Breathtaking bouquets, tasty delicacies, and even the odd salvage stall, selling human treasures that had been found on the ocean bottom. A mergirl could get lost in all the options.

But Peri knew exactly where she was going. She swam past the food and flower displays, over the organic sealife stalls, and around the tables of trinkets. She made straight for her favorite vendor. Paru's Pearls.

Pearls are plentiful under the sea, and many girls consider them ordinary. Plain. Common. To Peri they would always be the most beautiful things in all the oceans. She loved the way that some gleamed and others sparkled. They came in all the colors of the rainbow, from bright white to soft pink to inky gray to the blackest black she had ever seen.

She couldn't wait to browse the latest collection.

As she turned a corner, an older merwoman lost her grip on her shopping basket, sending a dozen live starfish tumbling across the aisle. Peri swerved out of the way as the woman dove after her lost bounty, then turned around to help. Most of the starfish remained within reach, and the woman quickly gathered them back. One made a gallant bid for freedom.

Peri retrieved the wayward starfish and returned it to the woman. "This one almost got away."

"Such a sweet dear." Her face crinkled into a bright smile. She reached up and pinched Peri's cheek. "Thank you."

Peri smiled back before turning and continuing toward her destination. The pearls called.

She approached the stall, swimming with such momentum that she stopped kicking and floated the rest of the way. If she hadn't been so excited, she might have noticed the trio passing in front of the stall.

Of course she had to crash hardest into the meanest of the three.

"I'm so sorry," Peri blurted, kicking herself out of the way, out of reach. "I wasn't looking where I was—"

"Swim much?" Astria asked, sneering.

"Yeah," Piper chirped. "Swim much?"

Venus snorted.

Peri stared wide-eyed at the terrible trio. Astria, Piper and Venus had been awful to her since guppihood. They took great delight in making her feel as small and worthless as possible. They tried to belittle Peri's best friend too, but Lily was the princess. They couldn't be as cruel with her or there might be repercussions. With Peri, though, they acted without restraint.

It didn't help that they were gorgeous. Astria had beautiful red hair and perfect alabaster skin. Piper looked more like a California mermaid, with sunny blonde hair and a fake tan that almost matched her golden tailfin. Venus was the most exotic, with dark skin, waves of midnight curls, and rich mahogany scales.

Peri felt dim in their presence. With her boring brown hair and brown eyes, she practically faded into the shadows. Only her tailfin, a bright copper in a thousand shining shades, made her feel special.

Looking down and away, Peri muttered another, "I'm sorry," and tried to swim past.

Astria never let her get away that easily.

"Shopping for pearls?" Her upper lip curled in a sneer. "Again?"

Peri just shook her head and darted into the stall. She heard them laughing and making fun as they swam off into the market. No matter how many times she told herself not to let them win, their barbs and mockery always stung.

Closing her eyes, she took a deep, cleansing breath.

"You're better than those three put together," a male voice said.

Startled, Peri spun around. Normally Paru worked her stall alone. Pearl harvesting is a time-intensive business and she couldn't spare any of her workers to hawk beads to tourists and shoppers when they could be gathering more. The merboy floating in front of her was most definitely not Paru.

It was her son.

He looked like a pirate. His hair, long and black as squid ink, was held back by a red and black scarf. Where it flowed out the back, she could see tiny silvery shells woven into his locks. She had never seen such dark eyelashes, and they framed pale silver eyes that glowed as they watched her. But it was his mouth, quirked up to one side, that she couldn't stop staring at.

"Wh-what?" she stammered.

He jerked his head after the terrible trio. "I've seen the likes of them plenty," he explained. "Your sort is worth ten of them." He winked. "At least."

Peri beamed. She couldn't help it, she grinned back. Lily always stood up for her, told her not to worry about petty mergirls. But Lily was her best friend. She was supposed to say that. This boy didn't even know her.

"Thanks," she said. Then, feeling more courage than usual, she held out her hand. "I'm Peri."

When his hand closed around hers, she felt sparks bursting all over her body.

"Riatus."

Riatus, she echoed in her mind.

He nodded over her shoulder as another shopper entered the stall. "Be right back," he said, looking into her eyes. "You'll wait?"

She nodded and he took off with a quick fin flick. Her hand felt cold without his warmth, but it wasn't empty. She looked down and saw, in the center of her palm, a pearl the size of a kelpberry. And the exact coppery shade of her tailfin.

Oh yes, she'd wait. She had a feeling she'd wait forever.

WHEN CORAL DREAMS

"Tonight is the night," Coral Ballenato promised herself as she studied her reflection in the mirror.

Her black curls rippled around her face in the gentle current that drifted through the window of her best friend's bathroom. The squid ink liner that made her dark brown eyes look even bigger than usual and the peachy stain she'd applied to her lips and cheeks—almost the same shade as her tailfin—made her feel prettier. Older. More confident.

And if she was finally going to make the first move with Zak Marlin, she needed to feel more confident. Way, way, way more confident.

"For the love of cod," Zanzia complained from beyond the bathroom door, "what is taking you so long?"

"Almost done," Coral called out.

One last check to make sure she hadn't overdone the makeup. It was one thing to give herself a little confidence-boosting makeover. It was another to make it so obvious that Zanzia noticed. The last thing Coral wanted was her best friend knowing how she felt about Zak.

Coral was just swiping off the excess color from her lips when she heard the front door open.

"I'm home," Zak called out, his voice resonating through the house.

She couldn't help the smile.

"Too bad," Zanzia shouted back, pretending to be annoyed when Coral knew good and well that she adored her big brother.

The first time Coral met Zak was when Zanzia invited her over to work on their Thalassinian Royal Family project in Year Seven history. Two years older than his sister, Zak was cute and charming and Coral fell for him instantly.

After three years she still hadn't managed to say anything more impressive than hello. But that was all going to change tonight. She was sixteen now—well, she would be on her birthday next month—and she was ready to take her crush to the next level. She'd been sitting at zero for so long that even an actual sentence would be a step up, but she was going all out. Before the night was over she would ask Zak out.

And hopefully she wouldn't faint when she did.

"Coral!" Zanzia jiggled the door handle. "Come on, I'm starving. Mom made calamari loaf."

"I'm coming," Coral said, yanking the door open.

"Finally." Zanzia grabbed her by the wrist before Coral could swim through. "Let's go."

For a mergirl about as big around as an electric eel, Zanzia had a never-ending appetite. Coral came over for family dinner every

Friday night and had seen her best friend put away an alarming amount of food. With her nerves always making her stomach swim circles, Coral could barely manage to eat half as much.

Zanzia dragged Coral downstairs to the kitchen so they could help set the table. Like she did every week, Coral started to set out five place settings.

"Here," Zanzia said, adding an extra set of dishes and seasticks to the stack.

Coral frowned. "I already have five."

"I know," Zanzia said with a wave. "Zak is bringing a friend over."

Coral shrugged. She was just setting down the sixth set of seasticks when Zak swam into the dining room.

She got so distracted that she floated into the edge of the table.

No matter how many times she saw him he always took her breath away. With his exotically golden skin and his dark gold hair, he looked like a piece of pirate treasure. His kelp-green eyes sparkled with mischief and his mouth stretched into a broader-than-usual smile, making a single dimple appear in his left cheek.

But as always, it was his tailfin that made him so very breath-stealing.

Where Zanzia's was pale lavender, her brother's tailfin was the deepest violet. Rich, luscious purple that made Coral want to trace her fingertips along the scales.

Tonight he looked even cuter than usual, with his golden curls tamed by some kind of gel and his standard tee traded in for a dress shirt.

She wanted to melt just being in the same room with him.

"Hey Zanzie," he said with a smile, knowing she hated the nickname. "Came back for more, Coral?"

Coral managed a smile. "Yes."

Always.

Zanzia swirled a plate toward her brother's head. He caught it easily and threw it back at her with a flourish. She stuck her tongue out at him as she set the plate on the table.

"Sea slug," Zanzia tossed over her shoulder as she swam back to the kitchen.

For a moment, Coral and Zak were alone in the dining room. This was her chance. Her opportunity to tell him, to ask him, to say... something. To ask him to the seaball game at school next week. That was her plan. No big deal, no strings attached. Just a simple date. Just ask.

But what came out was, "Um...."

Then, before she could even think of more words to add to that stellar start, there was a knock at the front door. Zak's eyes widened and he spun away, the biggest smile she had ever seen on his face.

Warning bells gonged in her mind. Puzzle pieces fell into place.

The extra seat at the table for Zak's friend.

His carefully groomed hair and dress shirt.

His huger than huge smile.

Coral watched with a sense of dread as Zak returned to the dining room with a beautiful mergirl at his side. She was obviously older than Coral, probably seventeen or eighteen, like Zak. Her long, flowing blond hair—so pale it was almost white—swirled around her like a net. The light from the overhead fixture glinted off the sequins on her ivory tank dress, making her look like a true angelfish.

"Coral, this is Angeliera."

Of course she was.

He shrugged his shoulder in a funny way, and Coral's gaze drifted down along his arm… to where he and the angelfish were holding hands.

"My girlfriend."

Coral's breath caught in her throat. She drifted into the table again, wrapped her hands around the back of a chair to hold steady.

A fin-flick later, Zanzia swam into the room, followed soon after by Mr. and Mrs. Marlin. As the family oohed and cooed over Zak's girlfriend, Coral kept herself from crying.

This wasn't the end of the world. The angelfish was his girlfriend. They weren't bonded for life or anything—yet.

Eventually it would end, and when that day came Coral would be ready. When Zak and the angelfish broke up, Coral would take the chance she'd been ready to take tonight.

And by then she would be the Coral she had always dreamed of being.

Dear reader,

Pretty in Pearls began as the very short story included at the end of this book, a 1000 word piece originally written for a mermaid magazine. When the timing didn't work for "Pretty in Pearls" to appear in the magazine, I turned that story in to a novella.

It was a story I had wanted to tell for a long time. While writing *Forgive My Fins*, Lily's best friend Peri was one of my favorite characters. She was loyal, smart, and had something secret in her past. I'm so glad I got to share more of her with you.

You may or may not know that sometimes I write books about non-mermaids. (Shhh, don't tell Lily!) If you want try those out, you can get the first two Darkly Fae books for free by going to:

TERALYNCHILDS.COM/GETFAE

I hope you loved reading about Peri and her pearly pirate as much as I loved writing about them. If you did, share your love by leaving a review or messaging me at *tlc@teralynnchilds.com*. Heck, be a rebel and do both!

About the Author

TERA LYNN CHILDS (*Authora neo*) is a newly discovered species of authorfish that always dreamed of being a mermaid, but never got closer than a career as a competitive swimmer. Loves to spend as much time as possible in and around water, right up until her fingertips turn all pruney, in the vain hope that one day her legs will magically turn into fins. When stuck on land, you can find *Authora neo* writing in coffee shops across the country, prowling for cool mermaid gear on Etsy, and creating the magical worlds of the Oh. My. Gods., Forgive My Fins, Sweet Venom, and Darkly Fae series. Find her online at *teralynnchilds.com*.

Made in the USA
Middletown, DE
17 June 2017